D0498527

MOURNER
AT THE DOOR

MOURNER
AT THE DOOR

STORIES

GORDON LISH

VIKING

VIKING
PUBLISHED BY THE PENGUIN GROUP
VIKING PENGUIN INC., 40 WEST 23RD STREET,
NEW YORK, NEW YORK 10010, U.S.A.
PENGUIN BOOKS LTD, 27 WRIGHTS LANE, LONDON W8 5TZ, ENGLAND
PENGUIN BOOKS AUSTRALIA LTD, RINGWOOD, VICTORIA, AUSTRALIA
PENGUIN BOOKS CANADA LTD, 2801 JOHN STREET, MARKHAM, ONTARIO,
CANADA L3R 1B4
PENGUIN BOOKS (N.Z) LTD, 182–190 WAIRAU ROAD, AUCKLAND 10,
NEW ZEALAND

PENGUIN BOOKS LTD, REGISTERED OFFICES:
HARMONDSWORTH, MIDDLESEX, ENGLAND

FIRST PUBLISHED IN 1988 BY VIKING PENGUIN INC.
PUBLISHED SIMULTANEOUSLY IN CANADA

ENTRIES HEREIN FIRST APPEARED IN RARITAN, THE ANTIOCH REVIEW, SOUTH-
WEST REVIEW, STORYQUARTERLY, CONFRONTATION, BOMB, THE LITERARY RE-
VIEW, THE MALAHAT REVIEW, ESQUIRE, CUTBANK, THE PENNSYLVANIA REVIEW,
BALCONES, WEBSTER REVIEW, NIT AND WIT, RIVERRUN, TRIQUARTERLY, COLUM-
BIA, AND WITNESS. CERTAIN OF THESE ENTRIES ALSO APPEARED IN PRIZE STORIES:
THE O. HENRY AWARDS, SUDDEN FICTION, AND THE PUSHCART PRIZE ANTHOLOGY.

LIBRARY OF CONGRESS CATALOGUING IN PUBLICATION DATA
LISH, GORDON.
MOURNER AT THE DOOR.
I. TITLE.
PS3562.I74.M6   1988   813'.54   87-40324
ISBN 0-670-82061-X

PRINTED IN THE UNITED STATES OF AMERICA
BY ARCATA GRAPHICS, FAIRFIELD, PENNSYLVANIA
SET IN BODONI

FOR BRODKEY, OZICK, DELILLO,
AND TO BARBARA,
FIRST, LAST, AND ALWAYS

. . . to keep a real and valued object in being.

FRANK KERMODE

Contents

THE DEATH OF ME   1

MR. GOLDBAUM   7

THE MERRY CHASE   17

SHIT   25

RESURRECTION   31

HISTORY, OR THE FOUR PICTURES
OF VLUDKA   39

THE LESSON WHICH IS SUFFICIENT
UNTO THE DAY THEREOF   43

CAN YOU TOP THIS?   49

THE WIRE   53

MR. AND MRS. NORTH   59

LAST DESCENT TO EARTH   63

THE TRAITOR   67

SPELL BEREAVEMENT 79

THE PROBLEM OF THE PREFACE 89

LEOPARD IN A TEMPLE 93

THE HILT 99

MY TRUE STORY 103

BALZANO & SON 105

THE FRIEND 109

AGONY 121

DON'T DIE 125

WHAT MY MOTHER'S FATHER
WAS REALLY THE FATHER OF 129

THE DOG 137

KNOWLEDGE 141

BEHOLD THE INCREDIBLE REVENGE
OF THE SHIFTED P. O. V. 145

ON THE BUSINESS OF GENERATING
TRANSFORMS 153

FISH STORY 155

It is reported that Wittgenstein's last words were these: "Tell them that I have had a wonderful life." Perhaps he did and perhaps he did not—have a wonderful life. But how could Wittgenstein have known one way or the other? As to a further matter, suppose those were not the words—suppose the words were German words. What I want to know is this—is it the same thing to have a wonderful life in another language? Or put it this way— if another language was the language that Wittgenstein had it in, then how could it have been a wonderful life?

———

MOURNER
AT THE DOOR

THE DEATH OF ME

I wanted to be amazing. I wanted to be so amazing. I had already been amazing up to a certain point. But I was tired of being at that point. I wanted to go past that point. I wanted to be more amazing than I had been up to that point. I wanted to do something which went beyond that point and which went beyond every other point and which people would look at and say that this was something which went beyond all other points and which no other boy would ever be able to go beyond, that I was the only boy who could, that I was the only one.

I was going to a day camp which was called the Peninsula Athletes Day Camp and which at the end of the summer had an all-campers, all-parents, all-sports field day which was made up of five different field events, and all of the campers had to take part in all five of all of the different field events, and I was the winner in all five of the five different field events, I was the winner in every single field event, I came in first place in every one of the five different

1

field events—so that the head of the camp and the camp counselors and the other campers and the other mothers and the other fathers and my mother and my father all saw that I was the best camper in the Peninsula Athletes Day Camp, the best in the short run and the best in the long run and the best in the high jump and the best in the broad jump and the best in the event which the Peninsula Athletes Day Camp called the ball-throw, which was where you had to go up to a chalk line and then put your toe on the chalk line and not go over the chalk line and then throw the ball as far as you could throw.

I did.

I won.

It was 1944 and I was ten years old and I was better than all of the other boys at that camp and probably all of the boys everywhere else.

I felt more wonderful than I had ever felt. I felt so thrilled with myself. I felt like God was whispering things to me inside of my head. I felt like God was asking me to have a special secret with him or to have a secret arrangement with him and that I had to keep listening to his secret recommendations inside of my head. I felt like God was telling me to realize that he had made me the most unusual member of the human race and that he was going to need me to be ready for him to go to work for him at any minute for him on whatever thing he said.

They gave me a piece of stiff cloth which was in the shape of a shield and which was in the camp colors and which had five blue stars on it. They said that I was the only boy

ever to get a shield with as many as that many stars on it.
They said that it was unheard-of for any boy ever to get as
many as that many stars on it. But I could already feel that
I was forgetting what it felt like to do something which would
get you a shield with as many as that many stars on it. I
could feel myself forgetting and I could feel everybody else
forgetting, even my mother and father and God forgetting.
It was just a little while afterwards, but I could tell that
everybody was already forgetting everything about it—the
head of the camp and the camp counselors and the other
campers and the other mothers and the other fathers and
my mother and my father and even that I myself was, even
though I was trying with all of my might to be the one person
who never would.

I felt like God was ashamed of me. I felt like God was
sorry that I was the one which he had picked out and that
he was getting ready to make a new choice and to choose
another boy instead of me and that I had to hurry up before
God did it, and that I had to show him that I could be just
as amazing again as I used to be and do something better
or at least something else.

It was August.

I was feeling the strangest feeling that I have ever felt. I
was standing there with my parents and with all of the
people who had come there for the field day and I was
feeling the strangest feeling which I have ever felt.

I felt like lying down on the field. I felt like killing all of
the people. I felt like going to sleep and staying asleep until
someone came and told me that my parents were dead and

that I was all grown up and that there was a new God in heaven and that he liked me better even than the old God had.

My parents kept asking me where did I want to go now and what did I want to do. My parents kept trying to get me to tell them where I thought we should all go now and what was the next thing for us as a family to do. My parents wanted for me to be the one to make up my mind if we should all go someplace special now and what was the best thing for the family, as a family, to do. But I did not know what they meant—do, do, do?

My father took the shield away from me and held it in his hands and kept turning it over and over in his hands and kept looking at the shield and feeling the shield and saying that it was made of buckram and felt. My father kept saying did we know that it was just something which they had put together out of buckram and felt. My father kept saying that the shield was of a very nice quality of buckram and was of a very nice quality of felt but that we should make every effort not to get it wet because it would run all over itself.

I did not know what to do.

I could tell that my parents did not know what to do.

We just stood around and people were going away to all of the vehicles that were going to take them to places and I could tell that we did not know if it was time for us to go.

The head of the camp came over and said that he wanted to shake my hand again and shake the hands of the people who were responsible for giving the Peninsula Athletes Day

Camp such an outstanding young individual and such a talented young athlete.

He shook my hand again.

It made me feel dizzy and nearly asleep.

I saw my mother and my father get their hands ready. I saw my father get the shield out of the hand that he thought he was going to need for him to have his hand ready to shake the hand of the head of the camp. I saw my mother take her purse and do the same thing. But the head of the camp just kept shaking my hand, and my mother and my father just kept saying thank you to him, and then the head of the camp let go of my hand and took my father's elbow with one hand and then touched my father on the shoulder with the other hand and then said that we were certainly the very finest of people—and then he went away.

MR. GOLDBAUM

Picture Florida.

Picture Miami Beach, Florida.

Picture a shitty little apartment in a big crappy building where my mother, who is a person who is old, is going to have to go ahead and start getting used to not being in the company of her husband anymore, not to mention not anymore being in that of anybody else who is her own flesh and blood anymore the instant I and my sister can devise good enough alibis to hurry up and get the fuck out of here and go fly back up to the lives that we have been prosecuting for ourselves up in New York, this of course being before we were obliged to drop everything and get down here yesterday in time to ride along with the old woman in the limo which had been set up for her to take her to my dad's funeral.

It took her.

It took us and her.

Meaning me and my sister with her.

Then it took us right back here to where we have been sitting ever since we came back to sit ourselves down and wait for neighbors to come call—I am checking my watch—about nine billion minutes ago.

Picture nine minutes in this room.

Or just smell it, smell the room.

Picture the smell of where they lived when it was both of them that lived, and then go ahead and picture her smelling to see if she can still smell him in it anymore.

I am going to give you the picture of how they walked—always together, never one without the other, her always the one in front, him always shuffling along behind her with his hands up on her shoulders, him always with his hands reaching out to my mother like that, with his hands up on her shoulders like that, her looking like she was walking him the way you would look if you were walking an imbecile, as if there was something wrong with the man, wrong with the way the man was—but there was nothing wrong with the way my father was—my father just liked to walk like that when he went walking with my mother, and my father never went walking without my mother.

I mean, that is what they did, that's how they did it when I saw them—that is what I saw when I saw my parents get old when I came down to Florida and had to see my old parents walk.

Try picturing more minutes.

I think I must have told you that we made it on time.

Only it was not anything like what I had been picturing when I had sat myself down on the airplane and started

8

keeping myself busy picturing the kind of funeral I was
going to be seeing when I got down to Florida for the funeral
my father was going to have.

Picture this.

It was just a rabbi that they went ahead and hired.

To my mind, he was too young-looking and too good-
looking. I kept thinking he probably had me beat in both
departments. I kept thinking how much he was getting paid
for this and would it come to more or would it come to less
than my ticket down and ticket back.

I felt bigger than I had ever felt.

I did not know where the ashes were. I did not know how
the burning was done. There were some things which I knew
I did not know.

But I know that I still felt bigger than I had ever felt.

As for him, he took a position on one side of the room,
the rabbi stood himself up on one side of the room, and me
and my sister and my mother, we all went over to where
we could tell we were supposed to go over on the other side
of the room, some of the time sitting and some of the time
standing, but I cannot tell you how it was that we ever knew
which one to do.

I heard: "Father of life, father of death."

I heard the rabbi say: "Father of life, father of death."

I heard the guy who was driving the limo say, "Get your
mother's feet."

Picture us back in the limo again. Picture us stopping
off at a delicatessen. Picture me and my mother sitting and
waiting while my sister gets out and goes in to make sure

they are going to send over exactly what we ordered when she called our order in.

Maybe it would help for you to picture things if I told you that what my mother has on her head is a wig of plastic hair that fits down over almost all of her ears.

It smells in here.

I can smell the smell of them in here.

And of every single one of the sandwiches that just came over from the delicatessen in here.

Now picture it like this—the stuff came hours ago and so far that is all that has. I mean, the question is this— where are all of the neighbors which this death was supposed to have been ordered for?

I just suddenly realized that you might be interested in finding out what we finally decided on.

The answer is four corned beef on rye, four turkey on rye, three Jarlsberg and lettuce on whole wheat, and two low-salt tuna salad on bagel.

Now double it—because we're figuring strictly half-sandwiches apiece.

Here is some more local color.

The quiz programs are going off and the soap operas are coming on and my sister just got up and went to go lie down on my mother's bed and I can tell you that I would go and do the same if I was absolutely positive that it wouldn't be against my religion for me to do it—because who knows what it could be against for you to go lie down on your father's bed—it could be some kind of a curse on you that for the rest of your life it would keep coming after you, until, ha ha, just like him, that's it, you're dead.

My mother says to me, "So tell me, sonny, you think we got reason to be nervous about the coffee?"

My mother says to me, "So what do you think, sonny, you think I should go make some extra coffee?"

My mother says to me, "I want you to be honest with me, sweetheart, you think we are taking too big of a chance the coffee might not be more than plenty of coffee?"

My mother says to me, "So what is your opinion, darling, is it your opinion that we could probably get away with it if I don't put on another pot of coffee?"

Nobody could have pictured that.

Nor have listened to no one calling and imploring us to hold everything, keep the coffee hot, that they are right this minute racing up elevators and down stairways and along corridors and will be any second knocking at the door because there is a new widow in the building and an old man just plotzed.

You know what?

I don't think that you are going to have to picture anything.

Except for maybe Mr. Goldbaum.

Here is Mr. Goldbaum.

Mr. Goldbaum is the man who sticks his head in at the door which we left open for the company which was on the way over.

Here is Mr. Goldbaum talking.

"You got an assortment, or is it all fish?"

That was Mr. Goldbaum.

My mother says, "That was Mr. Goldbaum."

My mother says, "The Mr. Goldbaum from the building."

Now you can picture a whole different thing, a whole different place.

This time it's the Sunday afterwards.

So picture this time this—my sister and me the Sunday afterwards. Picture the two different cars we rented to get out from the city to Long Island to the cemetery. Picture the cars parked on different sides of the administration building which we are supposed to meet at to meet up with the rabbi who has been hired to say a service over the box which I am carrying of ashes.

Picture someone carrying ashes.

Not because I am the son but because the box is made out of something too heavy.

Now here is a picture you've had practice with.

Me and my sister waiting.

Picture my sister and me standing around where the offices are of the people who run the cemetery, which is a cemetery way out on Long Island in February.

I just suddenly had another thought which I just realized. What if your father was the kind of a father who was dying and he called you to him and you were his son and he said for you to come lie down on the bed with him so that he could hold you and so that you could hold him so that you could both be like that hugging with each other like that to say goodbye before you had to actually go leave each other

and you did it, you did it, you got down on the bed with
your father and you got up close to your father and you
got your arms around your father and your father was
hugging you and you were hugging your father and there
was one of you who could not stop it, who could not help
it, but who just got a hard-on?

Or both did?

Picture that.

Not that I or my father ever hugged like that.

Here comes the next rabbi.

This rabbi is not such a young-looking rabbi, not such a
good-looking rabbi, is a rabbi who just looks like a rabbi
who is cold from just coming in from outside with the weather.

The rabbi says to my sister, "You are the daughter of
the departed?"

The rabbi says to me, "You are the son of the departed?"

The rabbi says to the box, "These are the mortal remains
of the individual who is the deceased party?"

Maybe I should get you to picture the cemetery.

Because it's the one where we all of us are getting buried
in—wherever we die, even if in Florida.

I mean, our plot's here.

My family's is.

The rabbi says to us, "As we make our way to the grave-
site, I trust that you will want to offer me a word or two
about your father so that I might incorporate whatever
ideas and thoughts you have into the service your mother
called up and ordered, may God give her peace."

Okay, picture him and me and my sister all going back

outside in February and I am the only one who cannot get his gloves back on because of the box, because of the canister—because of the motherfucking urn—which is too heavy for me to handle without me holding onto it every single instant with both of my hands.

The hole.

The hole I am going to have to help you with.

The hole they dug up for my father is not what I would ever be able to picture in my mind if somebody came up to me and said to me for me to do my best to picture the hole they make for your father's grave.

I mean, the hole was more like the hole which you would dig for somebody if the job they had for you to do was to cover up a big covered dish.

Like for a casserole.

And that is not the half of it.

Because what makes it the half of it is the two cinder blocks which I see are already down in it when I go to put down the urn down in the hole.

And as for the other half?

That's the two workmen who come over from somewhere I wasn't ready for anybody to come from and who put down two more cinder blocks on top of what I just put in the hole.

You know what I mean when I say cinder blocks?

I mean those blocks of gray cement or of gray concrete that when they refer to them they call them cinder blocks.

Four of those.

Whereas I had always thought that what they did was fill things back in with what they took out.

Unless they took cinder blocks out.

You can go ahead and relax now.

It is not necessary for you to lend yourself to any further effort to create particularities that I myself was not competent to render.

Except it would be a tremendous help for me if you would do your best to listen for the different sets of bumps the different sets of tires make when we all three of us pass over the little speed bump that makes sure cars go slow before coming into and going out of the cemetery my family is in.

Three cars, six sets of tires—that's six bumps, I count six bumps and a total of twenty-six half-sandwiches—six sounds of hard cold rubber in February of 1986.

Or hear this—the rabbi's hands as he rubs the wheel to warm the wheel where he has come to have the habit of keeping his grip in place when he puts his hands on the wheel to steer.

But who hears the rabbi think this?

"Jesus shit."

That's it. I'm finished. Except to inform you of the fact that I got back to the city not via the Queens Midtown Tunnel but via the Queensboro Bridge since with the bridge you beat the toll, that and the fact that I went right ahead and sat myself down and started trying to picture some of the things which I just asked you to picture for me, that and the fact that I had to fill in for myself where the holes were sometimes too big for anybody to get a good enough picture of them, the point being to get something written, to get anything written, and then get paid for it, this to cover the cost of Delta down and Delta back, Avis at their Sunday rate, plus extra for liability and collision.

One last thing—which is that no one told me.

So I just took it for granted that where it was supposed to go was down in between them.

THE MERRY CHASE

Don't tell me. Do me a favor and let me guess. Be honest
with me, tell the truth, don't make me laugh. Tell me, don't
make me have to tell you, do I have to tell you that when
you're hot you're hot, that when you're dead you're dead?
Because you know what I know? I know you like I know
myself, I know you like the back of my hand, I know you
like a book, I know you inside out. You know what? I know
you like you'll never know.

You think I don't know whereof I speak?

I know, I know. I know the day will come, the day will
dawn.

Didn't I tell you you never know? Because I guarantee
it, no one will dance a jig, no one will do a dance, no one
will cater to you so fast or wait on you hand and foot. You
think they could care less?

But I could never get enough of it, I could never get
enough. Look at me, I could take a bite out of it, I could
eat it up alive, but you want to make a monkey out of me,

17

don't you? You want me to talk myself blue in the face for you, beat my head against a brick wall for you, come running when you have the least little wish. What am I, your slave? You couldn't be happy except over my dead body? You think I don't know whereof I speak? I promise you, one day you will sing a different tune.

But in the interim, first things first. Because it won't kill you to do without, tomorrow is another day, let me look at it, let me see it, there is no time like the present, let me kiss it and make it well.

Let me tell you something, everyone in the whole wide world should only have it half as good as you.

You know what this is? You want to know what this is? Because this is some deal, this is some set-up, this is some joke. You could vomit from what a joke this is.

I want you to hear something, I want you to hear the unvarnished truth.

You know what you are?

That's what you are!

You sit, I'll go—I already had enough to choke a horse.

Go ahead and talk my arm off. Talk me deaf, dumb, and blind. Nobody is asking, nobody is talking, nobody wants to know. In all decency, in all honesty, in all candor, in all modesty, you have some gall, some nerve, and I mean that in all sincerity. The crust on you, my God!

I am telling you, I am pleading with you, I am down to you on bended knee—just don't get cute with me, just don't make any excuses to me—because in broad daylight, in the dead of night, at the crack of dawn.

You think the whole world is going to do a dance around you? No one is going to do a dance around you. No one even knows you are alive.

But if it is not one thing, then it is another.

Just who do you think you are, coming in here like a lord and lording it all over all of us? Do you think you are a law unto yourself? I am going to give you some advice. Don't flatter yourself—you are not the queen of the May, not by a long shot. Act your age—share and share alike.

Ages ago, years ago, so long ago I couldn't begin to remember, past history, ancient history—you don't want to know, another age, another life, another theory altogether.

Don't ask. Don't even begin to ask. Don't make me any promises. Don't tell me one thing and do another. Don't look at me cross-eyed. Don't look at me like that. Don't hand me that crap. Look around you, for pity's sake. Don't you know that one hand washes the other?

Talk sense.

Take stock.

Give me some credit for intelligence. Show me I'm not wasting my breath. Don't make me sick. You are making me sick. Why are you doing this to me? Do you get pleasure from doing this to me? Don't think I don't know what you are trying to do to me.

Don't make me do your thinking for you.

Shame on you, be ashamed of yourself, have you absolutely no shame?

Why must I always have to tell you?

Why must I always drop everything and come running?

19

Does nothing ever occur to you?

Can't you see with your own two eyes?

You are your own worst enemy.

What's the sense of talking to you? I might as well talk to myself. Say something. Try to look like you've got a brain in your head.

You think this is a picnic? This is no picnic. Don't stand on ceremony with me. The whole world is not going to step to your tune. I warn you—wake up before it's too late.

You know what? A little birdie just told me. You know what? You have got a lot to learn—*that's* what.

I can't hear myself talk. I can't hear myself think. I cannot remember from one minute to the next.

Why do I always have to tell you again and again?

Give me a minute to think. Just let me catch my breath.

Don't you ever stop to ask?

I'm going to tell you something. I'm going to give you the benefit of my advice. Do you want some good advice?

You think the sun rises and sets on you, don't you? You should get down on your hands and knees and thank God. You should count your blessings. Why don't you look around yourself and really see for once in your life? You just don't know when you're well off. You have no idea how the rest of the world lives. You are as innocent as the day you were born. You should thank your lucky stars. You should try to make amends. You should do your best to put it all out of your mind. Worry never got anybody anywhere.

But by the same token.

Whatever you do, promise me this—just promise me that you will do your best to keep an open mind.

What do I say to you, where do I start with you, how do I make myself heard with you? I don't know where to begin with you, I don't know where to start with you, I don't know how to impress on you the importance of every single solitary word. Thank God I am alive to tell you, thank God I am here to tell you, thank God you've got someone to tell you, I only wish I could begin to tell you, if there were only some way someone could tell you, if only there were someone here to tell you, but you don't want to listen, you don't want to learn, you don't want to know, you don't want to help yourself, you just want to have it all your own sweet way and go on as if nothing has changed. Who can talk to you? Can anyone talk to you? You don't want anyone to talk to you. So far as you are concerned, the whole world could drop dead.

You think death is a picnic? Death is no picnic. Face facts, don't kid yourself, people are trying to talk some sense into you, it's not all just fun and fancy free, it's not all just high, wide, and handsome, it's not just a bed of roses and peaches and cream.

You take the cake, you take my breath away—you are really one for the books.

Be smart and play it down. Be smart and stay in the wings. Be smart and let somebody else carry the ball for a change.

You know what I've got to do? I've got to talk to you like

a baby. I've got to talk to you like a Dutch uncle. I've got to handle you with kid gloves.

Let me tell you something no one else would have the heart to tell you. Look far and wide—because they are few and far between!

Go ahead, go to the ends of the earth, go to the highest mountain, go to any lengths, because they won't lift a finger for you—or didn't you know that some things are not for man to know, that some things are better left unsaid, that some things you shouldn't wish on a dog, not on a bet, not on your life, not in a month of Sundays?

What do you want? You want the whole world to revolve around you, you want the whole world at your beck and call? That's what you want, isn't it? Be honest with me.

Answer me this one question—how can you look me in the face?

Don't you dare act as if you didn't hear me.

You want to know what's wrong with you? This is what is wrong with you. You are going to the dogs, you are lying down with dogs, you are waking sleeping dogs—don't you know enough to go home before the last dog is dead?

When are you going to learn to leave well enough alone?

You know what you are? Let me tell you what you are. You are betwixt and between.

I'm on to you, I've got your number, I can see right through you—I warn you, don't you dare try to put anything over on me or get on my good side or lead me a merry chase.

So who's going to do your dirty work for you now? *You?* Do me a favor and don't make me laugh!

Oh, sure, you think you can rise above it, you think you can live all your life with your head in the clouds, in a cave, without rhyme or reason, without a hitch, without batting an eyelash, without blemish, without a leg to stand on, without fail, without cause, without a little bit of butter on your bread, but let me tell you something—you're all wet!

You know what? You're trying to get away with false pretenses, that's what! You think you're modesty itself, that's what! You think you look good in clothes, that's what! But you know what is wrong with you? Because I am here to tell you what is wrong with you. There is no happy medium with you, there is no live and let live with you, because talking to you is like talking to a brick wall until a person can break a blood vessel and turn blue in the face.

Pardon my French, but you know what I say?

I say put up or shut up!

Pay attention to me!

You think I am talking just to hear myself talk?

SHIT

I like talking about people sitting on toilets. It shows up in the bulk of my speech. Wherever at all in keeping with things, I try to work it in. You just have to look back at stories I have had printed to see that I am telling the truth. People on toilets is certain to show up with more than passing incidence. I will even go so far as to say that where you find a story with a person on a toilet in it, forget the name that's signed as author—no one but me could have written the thing. Indeed, it is inconceivable to me that I didn't.

But the one I've got now, this one here, it promises to be the best of the type.

Or anyhow the purest.

Well, the truest, then—the one with nothing in it made up.

The other thing about it that I like is that it could not be simpler to tell—nothing in it but just a man sitting on

a toilet in it and the wallpaper in it that the man is looking at.

Oh, of course—not just a man in general but me, in fact—
the one who is doing all of this telling right here this instant.

In fact, I would never tell a story about anyone else. For
one thing, it could never be true, could it? I mean, what
do I know about anyone else—or care to? Good Christ, I
have all I can do to marshal even a small enough interest
in myself.

Or do I mean large enough?

I don't know.

That's another thing I am always putting into stories—
"I don't know." Just those words, just like that. You see
a story with "I don't know" in it, that'll be your tip-off as
to who definitely wrote it. It could have anybody down there
under the title there as the one who did—but he didn't.

It's exciting. It is exciting.

Not writing, not speaking—but being a sneak.

When I was a boy, that was what I wanted to grow up
to be—a person who was an assassin and a sneak. I wanted
to be dangerous. That was when I was little.

When I was little, my mother would get me to sit on the
toilet and stay there and stay there until I could show her
something—and sometimes—more and more often—I
couldn't. She would say, "Put your royal bombosity down
on the throne and don't you dare let me see you get up
off of it until there is something in there in it for me to
look at."

It's terrible what I have to show for it now. I tell you, I don't know where the food goes. It's frightening. Am I getting poisoned?

I take things. You know—to make me go.

I especially take things when we go away and it gets worse—not going, the not-going. That's where this comes in—the story, this story, the wallpaper. Listen to this—I'd taken a lot of something—because it had been days already, days of nothing but of sitting and of not going, maybe even a week of it. So I'd swallowed enough to choke a horse, gone to bed, been down for mere minutes, when I had to get back up again and I really mean it, *get back up!* I mean, can't you just see me getting up? Fucking leaping?

It was somewhere quaint—an inn somewhere—you lose track—a cute hotel—meaning no bathroom of your own, meaning a bathroom out at the end of the hall, meaning a bathroom with a kind of a latch thing on the door—and a pitched ceiling pitched so low you had to keep bent over—even sitting down, I had to stay bent down—and even bent, I couldn't stop going—oh, God, just going and going—hours it felt like, gallons it felt like—it felt like my whole life was coming up—or out.

I mean out.

Which is when I started studying the wallpaper.

I thought I was sluicing away into death, dissolving from the inside out, rendering myself as shit, breaking down to basal substance, falling through the plumbing, perishing on a toilet that I could not even call my own.

You'll laugh, but I got scared.

27

.   .   .

I thought: "Call for help."

I thought: "Do it before you swoon."

Which is when I reached out for the wallpaper as you would for a lifeline, for a float.

I don't know.

I thought: "Hang onto the wallpaper."

I mean, with my mind, with that.

Well, I could see it was a wallpaper you could do it with— a pattern—growing things—things that grow—a picture of this, then of that—and the names.

Thus:

Blue-eyed grass.

Wintergreen.

Sweet William.

Sneezeweed.

Vetch.

Violet.

Primula.

Coreopsis.

Clover.

Mariposa.

Rose mallow.

Marsh marigold.

Dandelion.

Red-eye.

Clover.

Black-eyed Susan.

Poppy.

Blue bells.
Hepatica.
Buttercup.
Wood sorrell.
Belladonna.
Ivy.

I swear it—all those, each and every one.

Grasses, weeds—I don't know—crap, all that crap.

I sat there holding on.

I mean to tell you this—that I had had the thought that I was doing it for nothing less than life. Pretty dumb, right? After all, all it was was just a lot of shit. If anything, I should have been joyous, been jubilant, been pleased as punch. Hey, come on—I was going, wasn't I?

But I was scared to death.

I thought: "You think you're so smart, then make something out of this."

Skip it, what the facts are—I don't trade in science. I say that you just heard a story. I say your life, it saved your life.

RESURRECTION

The big thing about this is deciding what it's all about. I mean, by way of theme, what, what? Sure, it gives you the event that got me sworn off whiskey forever. But does that make it a tale of how a certain person got himself a good scare, put aside drunkenness, took up sobriety in high hopes of a permanent shift? I don't think so. Me, I keep feeling it's going to be more about Jews and Christians than about this thing of matching another man glass for glass. But I could be wrong in both connections. Maybe what this story is really getting at is something I'd be afraid to know it is.

Either way or whatever, it happened last Easter, which doesn't mean a thing to me because of me being Jewish. To my wife it's something, though, and I am more or less willing to play along—providing things don't get dangerously out of hand. Egg hunts for the kids, this is okay, and maybe a chocolate bunny wrapped in colored tinfoil. But I draw the line when it comes to a whole done-up basket. I don't see why that's called for, strands of candy-store grass getting stuck between floorboards and you can't get the stuff up even with a Kirby.

As for the Easter that I am talking about, not much of all of this was ever at issue. This was because we got invited out to somebody's place. I think the question just got answered this way—whatever they do, that'll be it, that'll be Easter—no reason for us to have to make any decisions. Which was a relief, of course—the whys and wherefores of which I am sure you do not need me to explicate for you. But my wife and I, we found something else to get into a fuss about, anyway. And that's the best I can do—say "something else." Because I don't remember what. Not that it was anything trifling. I'm certain it must have been something pretty substantial. I mean, aside from the whole routine thing of Easter.

But our boy got us reasonably jolly just in time for our arrival. What happened was, you just caught it from him, his thrill at getting into the country thing. You see, I think our boy really suffers in the city—I think my wife and I agree on this—not that you could ever actually get a confession of his agony out of him. He's all stoic, this kid of ours—God knows from what sources. Twelve years old and tough as a stump, though to my mind that is still nowhere near as tough as what I think you have to be. At any rate, he was out and gone as soon as we pulled up into the driveway. Trees, I guess. That boy, in him we're looking at a mighty passion to get up high on anything, his mother and his dad always hollering, "Come down from there! You're giving us heart trouble!"

The host and hostess, they were swell people. No need to say more. Nice folks. I was going to say "for Christians," but it is never necessary to actually say it, is it? As for the house-guest thing, we can skip right from Friday when we got there to Saturday before supper, them having over a few neighbors to meet us, three couples, more Christians. There was this one fellow among them, he seemed to take me for a person of special interest. We got to talking with what was surely more gusto than the rest. I don't know what about so much as I know it had to do with a lot of different municipal things—the houses around there, the gardening, getting the old estates up to snuff with strenuous renovations. There were these trays of Rob Roys going from hand to hand, and dishes of tiny asparagus spears and something lemony in a small porcelain bowl, kids underfoot, and the light in there was that country light, this burnished thing the April light can sometimes get to be at maybe five o'clock when you are indoors in a low-slung, high-gloss, many-windowed room. Well, I might as well tell you now, the fellow had a little girl there, maybe half the age of our boy. Harelipped—that was the thing—a girl with a bad face to go through life with, and I think I got drunk enough to say to the man, "Aw, God—aw, shit."

That's it. The story stops short right then and there where I am. Because the next thing I know, it's morning and I am waking up in one of the upstairs beds. But I cannot tell you how I got there. I cannot even tell you what was what between when I was having those Rob Roys and just standing there and when I was lying down and pulling away the comforter from my head.

There was a carillon across the street. Or across the town. Who knows? It was playing hymns. Or what I think are hymns. As for me, I felt entirely terrific—feeling nothing, not even a tremor, of what you would expect in the way of after-shocks. I mean, I had gotten so bad off that I had actually lost time, lost hours of real life. But there I was, waking up and never sprightlier, never more refurbished in fiber and spirit. Restored, I tell you—I could have said to you, "Look at me, for Christ's sake, look at me—I am in the pink!" Except for this thing of a whole night having vanished on me—that was something I wasn't going to think about yet—or didn't really actually even believe yet—whereas I kept trying to figure out how a thing like this sort of worked, one minute you're on your feet blazing away with a great new friend, the next minute you've skipped over no knowing what, and how did you get to here and to this from that and whatever that *was*?

Thing was, I knew I couldn't ask my wife. Christ, are you kidding? But I could smell the bacon down there, and went down, thinking that if I don't get a certain kind of a look, then this will mean I must have behaved passably enough, even if I was actually out like a light behind my eyes. And that's how the whole thing down there turned out, all of them downstairs—host, hostess, wife, our boys— and nobody—wife least of all—seeming to regard me as other than an immoderately late-riser and indecorous late-comer to the table.

Coffee is poured, conversation reinstalled.

But here is where the story stops short again. Because—just by way of making an effort to add myself to the civilities—I said, "Wretchedest luck, that guy, and such a handsome woman, his espoused, the two of them such a damnably attractive couple, and that little girl with the, you know, the thing, the lip." I mean, I did a speech as an offering, as a show of my harmless presence, the hearty closing up of the morning circle, the one we form to ward off night spells.

Not stops short enough, though. Because somebody was taking me up on it, converting ceremony to sermon. My wife, of course—her, of course—with that carillon going wild behind her. I tell you, whoever it was, and whatever he was playing, the man was good on the thing, the man was getting something colossal from those community bells.

But back to my wife, please—for she nips off a bit of toast and says, "You call that bad luck? Knowing what you know, how could you call that just a piece of bad luck, just a harelip?"

Ah, but this is madness, this is treachery—saying anything about a thing like this when I know it is a thing that ought to be left unsaid. Besides, we had no business being where we were. Even if it had meant keeping to the city and to squabbling over everything in sight, here is where we belong, where we should have stayed, where all the trees worth climbing are in a park. Those were rich people. My drink, when I was drinking, it had never been anything too mixed.

I mean, what the hell was she getting at, just a harelip?

I didn't give her the satisfaction. I didn't ask. What I did was go to work on it with my own good sense—trying harder to remember, or to make things up—the result being that on the way home, I came up with a thing that goes roughly like this—the fellow with the little girl sort of producing himself from out of the midst of the rest, me not tracking his features any too clearly, my vision already diminished by at least half.

"Ah, yes," he says, and with his glass he gives my glass a click. He says, "Great to meet the neighbors, don't you say?" He says, "See the fucking neighbors?" He says, "Here's to fucking us."

And me, what did I do? Say *l'chaim*? Click his glass back?

"Oh, sure, sure," I hear him say. "Sure, sure—right, right—fine, fine—good, good—swell, swell."

I know. We drank.

Did I ever say, "Surgery can handle that"? Is that what I said? Or "It's nothing—a good man can fix that right up"?

I mean, what had I said to him to get him to say to me, "Had a little chap of his measure once," and lift his Rob Roy in salute to my boy? Except that I am just guessing that he was doing that—because by then it was too hard for me to see if the man was really pointing anybody out. "Bloody garage door took his fucking head off, don't you see? No, really, old chap. Brand new electric sort of a thing. Electronic, I mean."

We were coming up on a toll-booth, my wife and I. In real life, that is. But I don't have to tell you that I wasn't there with all my wits. "Take this!" my wife was saying, and I took a hand off the wheel to take the coins from her hand, meanwhile still making up sentences to keep filling in the blanks.

"Nothing against the old homestead, though—no fucking hard feelings."

That's what I think the man said next. Or something like, "The fucker drops like a shot the day they finish getting the wiring up."

I don't think I ever got his name, the man who came for cocktails when the neighbors came over and who then left so that the hostess could finally sit us down to something— my wife says cold lamb. She also says she was standing right there and heard every single word, him saying how they'd lost a son but that God had made it up to them with the girl. My wife says the man said to me, "I'd spotted you, you know," and that I said, "For what?" and that the man said, "For a Jew."

But maybe my wife was making that up, too, just the way that I am making this up, especially the part about me hearing the sonofabitch say, "Happy fucking Easter," and me seeing myself get a hand up out of my pocket to hold his chin in place so that I could aim for right on his lips when that was where I kissed him.

So for what it's worth, that's the whole story, and notice who just told it cold-sober.

HISTORY,
OR THE FOUR PICTURES
OF VLUDKA

He said that he had been considering the convention of the
Polish girl, and I said, "In literature—you mean in literature," and he said, "Yes, of course," how else would he
mean? touching eyeglasses, beard, lip while noting that he
was feeling himself compelled to take up the pose of the
poet in eucharistic recollection of etc., etc., etc.—as literary
necessity, that is.

He said, "So can you help, do you think?"

I said, "From memory, you mean."

"That's it," he said. "Any Polish girl you ever had a
thing with."

I can tell you what the trouble with me was—no beard
anywhere on me, no eyeglasses either, meat of real conse-
quence to neither of my lips—nothing, at least, to speak
of, nothing to give me a good grab of anything, nothing on
my face for anyone to hang onto, nothing to offer even me
a good grip.

He said, "Whatever comes to mind, I think."

Here was the thing with me—I did not know what to do with my hands.

"Whatever pops into your head," he said, off and at it again, fingering eyeglasses, beard, lip.

The oaf was all feelies, I tell you—the moron was ledges from stem to stern.

"So," he said, "anything you might want to conjure up for me, then? I mean, just the barest sketching, of course, no need for names, as it were, and addresses."

But I had never had one. I mean, I hadn't had a Polish girl. What I had had back before that inquiry had come to me was a great wanting to pass myself off as a fellow who had had whatever could be got.

"Vludka," I said, "her name was Vludka."

"Perfect," he said. He said, "Name's Vludka, you say."

"Yes," I said, "and very, for that matter, like it, too."

"I see her," he said. "Stolid Vludka."

"In the extreme," I said. "In manner and in form."

"Yes, the nakedness," he said. "A certain massiveness, I imagine—wide at the waist, for instance, the effect of flesh built up in slabs."

I said, "Vludka's, yes. And hard it was, too. Oh, she was tougher and rougher than I was, of course—morally and physically the bigger, better party."

"But smallish here," he said, showing.

I said, "Even said she was sorry about it for the way they were before she took her clothes off, and then when she had them off, saw that what she should have been warning me about was about how big everything else was."

He said, "Could tell you'd be lost inside her, awash in stolid Vludka, mouse proposing monkey business to elephant."

I said, "There I was, a punk in spirit, a puniness in fiber."

He said, "It was impossible."

"I said to her, 'Vludka, this is impossible.' "

He said, "She was too Polish for you, much too Polish."

"So I said to her, 'Do something, Vludka. Manage this for us.' "

He said, "She was pliant, compliant—Polish. You said to her, 'You handle it, Vludka, and I'll watch,' and she did," he said, "didn't she?"

"Because she was pliant," I said. "Compliant," I said. "Polish," I said.

He said, "It took her eleven minutes."

I said, "I sort of knew it would."

He said. "That's how stolid she was."

I said, "It was endless. My arm was exhausted for her. I timed her on my watch. Even for a Polish girl, it was incredible. I tell you, she used a blunt fingertip, a thumb even."

"It was ponderous," he said. "Thunderous," he said. "You thinly watching, you meagerly urging. 'For pity's sake, come, Vludka, come!' "

· · ·

41

What I didn't tell him is that what I was really watching were the four pictures of Vludka on Vludka's bedroom wall instead.

These are what they were of—of Vludka at the railing of a big wooden-looking boat, of Vludka in a runabout with her hands up on the wheel, of Vludka and her father on a blanket in a forest, of Vludka squatting on a scooter near a road sign that when Vludka finished doing it to herself she said, "Majdanek, you know what's there?"

He said, "Well?"

I said, "Well what?"

He said, "What you were thinking—the road sign—Majdanek—what was it that was there?"

I said, "You read my mind."

He said, "No. Just the standard stuff about the camps."

All my life I have never known what to do with my hands. Except for shit like this.

THE LESSON
WHICH IS SUFFICIENT UNTO
THE DAY THEREOF

Have I not been insisting it is the most instructive of stories?
In fact, it is the most instructive of stories. Indeed, the great
thing will be to see if I can uncover the core of the instruction
that is prospectively in it. I mean, in the telling, maximize
the teaching—do it, and keep on doing it, from the beginning to the end.

As to what I am talking about, it concerns an apple and
an apple tree, the one having fallen from the other.

Not that that is all that there is to it. I mean, there are
people, there are things. But who has the patience for even
the surfaces of these?

Here is the bitter truth.

You have to have the patience of a saint.

Whereas I do not even have the patience of a Lish.

But I should say of a Lishnofski, not of a Lish.

Considering.

Considering the name Lish doesn't point to where I meant
to. It doesn't point to the tree I fell from.

. . .

Listen to me talk in metaphor!

Isn't that always the way? One minute, making excuses for yourself—the next minute, making life miserable for everybody else.

It's hopeless.

Let's be honest with each other, I am already exhausted from just this much of it—the story of anything, even the story of Gordon Lishnofski.

But there I go again, piling figuration upon figuration. For one thing, Gordon just stands for Morton—and exhaustion, for another, for boredom.

Or nobody calling or coming around to say hi, hello, aren't you swell.

God, you get so fed up with speech.

Just the idea of telling anybody anything is enough to make you sick, every word weighing tons more than it did the last time you said it—or saw it—or heard it—or wrote it—or thought it. Who's got the energy? Who's got the strength? That's why the apple falls off the tree—from such a heaviness from life, from what's holding it getting weak.

But silence is a tiresomeness, too.

That's what my dad's was, by the way. He was a wordless one, I can tell you. No one came any more wordless than my dad did. But it was a shout to you if you were his son.

You know what his favorite word was?

Atrocious.

Putrid and *vile*, he liked those ones, too.

He'd say, "These stringbeans are atrocious," and for the whole rest of the meal he would say not one other thing at all.

Or he would say, "These stringbeans are vile," or "These stringbeans are putrid."

It never occurred to me until right this minute that maybe that's what they incontestably were. I mean, when I was there at the family table, did I ever sample any of the vegetables? Who knows, maybe vile and so on, maybe these were even mild complaints insofar as denunciations of my mother's canned vegetables should have gone.

Considering.

Considering my mother couldn't actually cook anything any good anyhow.

It was just that I didn't care if she couldn't. You're a kid, you do not much care about much other than the fewest of foods.

Bananas—I loved bananas—and olives and crackers—and licorice, licorice was eating breath.

You know how my father would eat an apple? You want to hear how my father would eat an apple? Get a bite off of it and chew it and chew it and then hold under his chin the hand that holds the apple, and spit into it, spit into the hand, spit into it nothing but the chewed-up skin.

I used to think he could do it because of his teeth, or

because of his gums, or because of his tongue—or because he had a harelip and talked nyike nyis.

It scared me silly—a man eating an apple like that, a man nyalking nyike nyis.

Hey, where did I all of a sudden get all this get-up-and-go from? To speak with such vim and vigor with!

Considering.

Considering that I have been trying so hard to get across the impression that I absolutely do not give a shit.

So what do you think—fact or fiction, Morton Lishnofski?

I wonder what it would have felt like, kissing a person with a harelip. Kissing the person right where the harelip is, just imagine it! All I can say is, praise be that in my house we had a host of rules set up to keep the spectre of contagion at bay, or in check. Wiping off the mouthpiece of the telephone with anything disinfectant, there was one of them for you—and kissing someone on the cheek, there was a second.

I can't think of a third.

Sorry, mind's not on what I'm saying, I think.

So which was it, Pine-Sol or Breath O'Pine?

I don't know about you—but me, I have had enough of this. I mean, how much is it they expect a man to take? Considering, of course.

Considering today's another Father's Day.

Considering that here I am having to sit here and say all of this.

It's nyile and nyutrid, isn't it?

Apples falling at all, and then where, where they fall— when they do.

CAN YOU TOP THIS?

Listen to me, there are two hippopotamuses standing in a
river, such a filthy dirty river, it is horrible, it is simply
horrible, and the sun, my God, you would not believe it,
you just would not believe it, what with the heat and the
sun and with how sticky and humid and muggy it is, it is
stifling, it is absolutely unbelievable how stifling, it is positively beyond all believability, a day so stifling like this, a
day which could kill you like this, a day which could do
away with you with just one hour, one minute, one breath,
but meanwhile all day long, from when the sun comes up
in the morning to when the sun is going down at night, all
day long the two hippopotamuses are standing there in the
scorching water like that, they are up to their ears and their
eyeballs in the scorching torpid water like that, and it is
this filthy dirty hot disgusting water like that, not either
one of them moving a single muscle in it, the two of them
not budging, not even one inch, not even leaning a fraction
of an inch in this direction or in that direction, except for

49

maybe if you want to count these little tiny twitches of the
eyelids, of the ears, these little tiny trembles you would
probably call them, these little trembles and twitches, but
otherwise the two hippopotamuses are like granite, like stone,
standing there in the disgusting water from first thing in
the morning to the time when it is almost sundown, all day
long the two of them all covered up by the filthy hot torpid
dirty water like that except for just where their little ears
are sticking up out of it and constantly twitching little twitches
and their big bulgy eyes are poking up a little bit out of the
water and the eyelids, you can see that the eyelids are giving
these little bitty trembles, these tiny little trembles, these
little tiny tremblings, maybe from flies probably or maybe
from little nits or from something even tinier than that, or
it could be from some kind of teensy almost invisible things
which like to creep around on the eyelids of hippopotamuses—but barring this, barring the twitches of the ears
and the twitches of the eyelids, the two hippopotamuses are
just standing there and standing there and you could not
even see them breathing, and the water meanwhile just goes
gurgling all around them like it is some kind of filthy dirty
torpid syrup probably, more like it is torpid ooze than it
is anything like even water even, more like it is some kind
of special water which can get totally exhausted, and this
is it, this is how it is, this is how the whole situation is from
just after when the sun first came up in the morning to
almost when it is getting good and ready to go down again
at night, which is when one of the hippopotamuses, which
is when the hippopotamus which is the slightly older hip-

popotamus and the slightly more overweight hippopotamus, which is when this hippopotamus all of a sudden moves his little feet a little tiny bit and more or less just gets them moved into place into a somewhat slightly new position, and then he opens his eyelids all of the way and looks around a little bit and he says, "I don't know—all day long I still can't get it through my head that today is a Tuesday."

No, he says, "It's such a crime just to stand?"

No, wait a minute, she said he says, "Who can think, a thing like this? Can anybody collect his thoughts?"

The truth is this—I don't really remember what the punchline was. But I don't suppose I have the other part much more faithfully recorded, either. You see, I think I was pretty jumpy when I heard it, plus I know that I was too young to be old enough to listen when big things were probably being said. The only thing that I have for more than thirty years been sure of is that my Aunt Adele told jokes when the cancer started going from her bladder to her bones, that and the fact that my Aunt Adele kept calling up to my house from Miami to New York to tell lots of different jokes to whoever was home. Of course, it was always my mother who was home—my mother, so far as I can remember, always was. But I picked up the downstairs phone once, and heard something for myself on the order of what you just heard, plus the power of two women laughing as a boy listens in.

THE WIRE

My wife says, "Look at you. Just look at you. How can you
look like that? Why don't you take a good look at yourself?
Look at me, don't you have any idea of what you look like?
What do you think people are going to think when they
look at you? Tell me, how can you go around looking like
that? Do you know what you look like? You couldn't conceivably know what you look like. Who would believe that
anyone could look like that? I can't believe what you look
like. It's hard for me to grasp it, a man who can go around
looking like what you look like. What is the matter with
you, don't you know what you look like? You probably
don't have the first idea of what you look like. You act like
you're completely oblivious to what you look like. Don't
you realize that people are looking at you? Have you no
conception of the fact that people are looking at you? Why
are you so utterly unaware of the fact that you cannot go
around looking like whatever you happen to feel like look-

ing like? Take a look at yourself. Just go ahead and take just one good look."

That's what my wife says.

As for myself, I used to think it didn't put her in the best of lights to be saying it.

Years ago there was a fellow who kept trying to offer me some observations along the very same lines of the ones which my wife, in her time, does. But I didn't see any reason to argue with him, either. So far as his story goes, he's dead as a doornail now, so let's just get his name and address right out here on this sheet of paper here—Johns, John Bernard Johns, his conduct of the business of psychiatry being carried out by him at 150 East 57th Street.

Here's an example of it.

"Just look at yourself. Just go look at yourself. Why don't you come to your senses and just take a good look at yourself?"

But I have always been the sort of person to take a different view of looking.

You take today on the subway, for instance, the woman with the immense suitcase . . .

Here is what my mother used to say to me:

"Do you see what you look like? I don't think you see what you look like. How can you let people see you looking like that? You want to go through life seeing yourself looking like that?"

Look, the man committed me and made sure I stayed

right where he did it to me, and this was for just shy of twelve awful months.

I kept trying to see up her pants past where the crease was.

I'm leaving out everything. I'm leaving out even the highlights of it. I'm just too tired of it to ever go over the whole history of it again.

All right, it was eight months, not twelve months—but since when is time the point?

He said to me, "It's high time you took the time to take a decent look at yourself."

Here is what happened on the E train today—the woman the color of what do they say? There is a woman the color of coffee with cream in it, and she's got on short pants on her, and for the top she's got on what I think they call a halter top, and they're both that look you will sometimes see of their being both at the same time just tight enough and just loose enough, and she has got her hair mown all the way down to her skull to a woolly-looking furzy high-domed cuntlike frizzle of a thing and there her legs are, uncovered and glowy right up to almost past her backside almost and crossed in the manner of how only a woman who is this lovely ever crosses them—and the eyes and the arms and the mouth and the throat! I mean those things of her.

Aren't you supposed to say one-fifty when someone writes 150?

She had a small child up on one shoulder.

She was about twenty, and it was—I don't know—maybe it was a baby.

There wasn't any ring on her finger.

The child, the baby, it was out like a light in any light, and I could tell that the mother was almost also.

Oh, well, yes—I could see the slenderest of gold ones.

Like a wire.

But it wasn't on that finger.

My sister used to say to me: "I don't think you ever stop to think of just what you look like."

The building I live in now, it's so full of psychologists and psychiatrists and psychoanalysts, it isn't even funny.

This whole block is.

They know who Johns is here.

Or who Johns was.

His fame went all the way up from 57th Street—or, if the rhyme's all the same to you, came up—because here is where I live up here now.

The suitcase, just to look at it—you could just look at it and tell it weighed a ton.

The first girl I ever tried to get to do it, she did it—but she didn't look like anything, and neither have any of the others of them all of the times ever since.

Hundreds.

Thousands.

Not one fucking one!

But what about the girl on the E today when I was going for the D at Seventh?

You've got a perfect right to know why the man committed me, but who wants to speak ill of the dead?

I thought: "Someone's dumped her. She's got no one. God has sent me this deliverance."

The first girl I ever did it with was probably better to look at than the second one was. Right then and there you could tell the pattern was going to lock in like iron right from then and there to as long as I ever lived.

The last one said: "Okay, but do not think that you are fooling me with what you look like, buster, not even for one lousy minute."

I thought: "Wouldn't it be proof of heaven's handiwork if she gets out at Seventh to also change over for the D?"

He said it with the accent on the *nard*.

Dead at forty-three.

Heart.

Heaven was taking a hand in it, all right—except only up to a point it was. Because when she got it to the door, struggling with it and with the baby so bad that it made you want to kill for love, what she said to me was "No" when I said "You want me to help you with it so you can get it down the stairs?"

I'm not telling the whole story.

Tomorrow is June 17th.

Seventeenth.

The whole story is, she said she wasn't going down the stairs, but when I got down them and looked back up them, there she was, coming down them and then going right past me on the platform and all the way away from me to the end of the platform as far as she could get, that cargo of her wretchedness notwithstanding.

My wife said, "Who do you think is ever going to look at you looking like that?"

Hey, but guess whose sister the motherfucker was humping when his ticker up and jumped him forty bucks into a one-hundred-dollar hour of friendly family psychotherapy!

Yeah, but lately, lately, what I'd like to know is this: Who has the one true love of my life ever been doing to death for me, *no es verdad?*

MR. AND MRS. NORTH

"Yuh, yuh, yuh."

"Oooo. Uuuu. Uuumach."

This is how they wake up. They wake up vomiting. Actually, it is a little after they wake up that Mr. and Mrs. North commence to vomit.

They are not fools.

They know as well as you do the large peril of vomiting in one's sleep. Even in a condition of light sleep, there is the risk of choking to death on some chunk of what gets thrown up from the stomach. The odd bolus of ingestimenta could skid back and lodge itself in some cute contour of the food pipe. Even with pillows lifting the head, you're taking a chance if you sleep on your back.

Mr. and Mrs. sleep on their backs. Once abed, that is the posture each pursues throughout the course of the night.

They are good sleepers.

They do not vomit until they wake up.

They have separate bathrooms. Mr. and Mrs. use separate bathrooms for the act of vomiting. True, they could both in fact hasten themselves to the nearer bathroom, the one spouse disgorging himself into the sink while the other knelt before the toilet.

Don't ask me why that's not the way they do it.

Perhaps in some families vomiting is a private matter. Or perhaps it is that in this family each of the parties favors the same species of receptacle—Mr. and Mrs. being, after all, husband and wife and therefore alike. Without my speaking of it too descriptively, the duration of their relation might have made of them a pair of sink-vomiters or of toilet-vomiters or even of tub-vomiters, vomiters whose habit it is to vomit into the same class of concavity.

See what you can make of this.

Early in the marriage they kept mixing bowls at the ready—his on his side, hers on hers—on the floor by their bed. But as the marriage matured, its principals managed to scale ever greater elevations of self-control—thus making, in the end, the practice of installing the nearby catch-basin superfluous to their needs.

Just as well. For the bowls were notably unsightly seen squatting there to either side of the bed, where company might spot them when company was taken on a tour of the Northern family residence.

"What's that?" the attentive guest might think to himself—and, receiving no answer to the unstated question, presume the worst.

So the mixing bowls were set aside, and it was a welcome

triumph when they were, for now neither Mr. nor Mrs. has
to cope with the nuisance of collecting such clumsy utensils
from the kitchen night after cantankerous night. Sad to
say, they had, in the old days, now and then quarreled on
this score, but only on those occasions when they had both
already retired for the evening, having neglected to situate
their bowls in place beforehand. First he, and then she, or
first she, and then he, would claim fatigue much too fan-
tastic to undertake the tiring trip all that mileage to the
kitchen.

He, for example, would say, "I'm just too weary to do
it, my darling," whereupon she would say, "That goes double, my love, for me."

Yet someone clearly had to, and, in the course of things,
much as it was contrary to their natures, a fearful squabble
would ensue until one or the other relented—which one
being neither here nor there.

Thankfully, the debate over the mixing bowls became, in
its time, a thing of the past. What remained to be ironed
out was this—who was to have exclusive use of the nearer
bathroom? It was vexatious, this question. Naturally neither Mr. nor Mrs. proved willing to concede that he was
any the less in control of his vomitus. To be sure, it seemed
unfair that one or the other should have to lose a point to
win another. So it fell out between them that it was quite
properly the Mr. who ought travel the greater distance—
since this seemed to them the chivalrous, and therefore the
more romantical, resolution.

He said he could be happy with this program, and indeed

he proved to be—for it pleased him to act in a fashion that promoted his self-esteem, and she, for her part, was happy that her presence created the opportunity for him to carry out those gestures of courtly conduct consistent with his status as he understood it to rank, a generosity that enhanced *her* self-esteem since she, in effect, was providing for his.

But as to the present, so that you might hear for yourself.

As a rule, the spouses greet one another before they start to vomit—a hale "Good morning, dearest," or some such expression of politesse and neighborly affection. It might even happen that a number of sentences will have passed between the parties before one or the other of them is overcome by the first familiar spasm.

The following passage is drawn from their jointly reported account.

"Good morning, my dear."

"Good morning to you."

"Sleep well, my sweet?"

"Ever so well, thank you. And you?"

"Oh, fine, thank you. Very well indeed."

"That's good. Good, good, goo-uh, goo-*uh*. Uh. *Yuh*."

"Uuuu. *Uuuuuch*."

"Yuh, yuh, ooyuch, *yach*."

"Uuuuuch. Uuuuuch. Ooooo*wach*."

And so on and so on, a connubial symphony, an excellence, the matchless accord of the seasoned adventure in the monogamy of furious dreamers.

LAST DESCENT TO EARTH

Must be my third time around this time. Or is one supposed to say *round*? Not that I am claiming that that's such a lot, just the three tries, and one of them not even plausibly that yet, not even decently enough of a try so far that I could quit it right here and still get to count it as anything much more than the start of a start. Great Christ Almighty, there used to be a time when one could slog one's way through twenty, thirty, forty of the kind, knocking one's fnocking brains out over some adverb-ridden thing, proud as punch to have turned one's nose up at as many as that many words. Ah, but Great Christ Almighty, my friends, your parts-of-speech were no big deal back then.

One had words galore.

One had words to burn.

One had to beat them off with a stick.

I myself had words to kill, and did away with as many as one could.

Oh, there were sentences to go around back then, and don't let anybody ever tell you different.

Unless he says *round*, that I should have said *round*, that actually it's *round* which would have been the proper way to do it.

My pal Denis says that one of the things which Nietzsche once said was a thing which went roughly along the lines of the idea of this:

"What good did killing God do us if, when all is said and done, grammar still lives and breathes?"

Listen, you think anybody ever needs to be told?

Speaking of which—not of Him or of Denis but just of listening—there is this one fellow who is sitting listening to this other fellow in the two earlier times around when I made the two earlier tries at the story which I am fixing to tell you for the third time here, just like it right this minute is now with you, please God, sitting listening to me.

Except they're both on a plane.

On an airplane.

Which has been going around and around because it can't get in.

It is a question of congestion.

Or of round and around.

You have to have a runway, you have to have clearance, the traffic is terrific, you think it takes a genius to invent such a thing as this?

Or to tell you how scared to death it is so easy for everyone to get when we have gone from here to there but the pilot cannot get in?

Save your breath.

Who hasn't been through it?

One's belted down into the last seat one's going to ever get to sit in—while meanwhile the lummox keeps wallowing the fnock around, no clarification from the fnocking cockpit forthcoming!

So it's no wonder, is it?

That you'll talk just to hear yourself talk—as one of the men on the plane in the story did. Or in the story on the plane.

Like this:

"Would you believe it if I told you that I travel with the dead? No, really, it is actually a business, I am with a firm that is in this business, you sometimes have to have somebody with it if there is a casket which is in transit, either because it is a statute, either because it is probably a state or federal statute, or because of the airlines themselves enacting it, a regulation which they themselves have deemed enacted."

Oh, you could look to me to be talking my head off just as frantically as he is if it was me who was strapped in up there next to the fellow we just sat here and heard—what with nothing by way of a word from the people in charge of the thing and still no hint of the first descent to earth.

But I'm down here writing—and going for my third.

Whereas up there, in that airplane, the man next to the man just listens.

Or appears to.

So the fellow talking keeps talking.

This is some more of what he says.

"You have to be bondable."

"What if it's really the wheels?"

"You think they're just killing the fuel so as to keep the conflagration to a minimum?"

Hey, I know how the fnocker feels.

They should really have to tell you. Even when it's just routine, I think they should have to keep issuing updates and reassurances, wising you up as to the fact that you are not just going around and around for no reason at all or, Great Christ Almighty, around when it should be round.

So what's the story?

Go ahead and try for four?

My pal Denis just took off for Ireland, whereas Nietzsche couldn't sit tight, couldn't stay put, after Basel.

THE TRAITOR

They looked to me to be Tibetan or Mongolian or—I don't
know, I just want to say it—Burmese. Oh, but this is terrible. This is embarrassing. Really, there's not a blessed
thing I know about national types like those, about what
they're supposed to look like or what you'd call them if you
knew. I mean, maybe this couple had actually looked to me
mostly like they came from Thailand, but I didn't know
how to say it, so I right away gave up the thought because
I could see ahead, see the situation of the adjective coming,
and knew it would have me stumped, frontwards, back-
wards, and sidewards, knew it would have had me whipped
hands-down. Thailander? Thailander can't be right. At least
I would not bank on my ever having heard anyone say it—
say Thailander. Great day, you'd know it if you'd ever
heard anyone say it. But neither can I imagine what you
might conceivably say instead, unless it's Thai*land*ian, which,
now that I have actually said it, sounds to me excessively
improbable and possibly insulting.

You may as well know that I once got into some absolutely dreadful trouble over a thing like that—from referring to a certain person by this name rather than by that name. Or it may have been the other way around. Frankly, it was not all that long ago, this misunderstanding. It remains to be proved, in fact, which, if either, was the case—that I misunderstood or was misunderstood. Not that the couple on the subway represented the opportunity for the same sort of confusion. Oh, no, theirs was a confusion of an entirely different sort. I mean, you could see that they were not the kind of people to care a fig for how anyone anywhere might elect to propose a designation of them. Or do I mean something simpler and can't say it? But I am a man of action, you see, and not, as you will also see, of words. Although I doubtlessly know more about words than would most persons of my ilk.

Dropped a stitch back there. Had meant to say that these two—the man and the woman—looked to me as if they had reached what is sometimes called "a higher state."

To be absolutely candid with you, I just don't know how I got us into this Thailand thing. Actually, the more I behold the question, the more I am willing to favor the notion that they, the couple, were very likely Siberian, by which I mean the man and woman who were sitting across from me on the subway last week. Ah, but I forget, I forget—so bundled up against the cold they were, not on your life could they really have been Siberian on a bet. Unless, of course, I am making the mistake of believing that where you come from has something substantive to do with how

you react to what the temperature is where you go to. On
the other hand, who's to say one hasn't issued from Siberian
parentage but was nonetheless native to somewhere else
where one might grow up warm?

Except they didn't look that way. Not to me, at least. To
me, they looked like people who had gotten used to living
in measureless wretchedness and then unused to it. You
know what they looked like to me? They looked like people
who were freezing in New York.

But you must know how everyone will look just this very
way to you when you see them on the subway and it is
winter in New York. Think of books nobody ever really
reads but which by our age who cares if they catch you at
it. At not having done it, I mean. Me, too, I didn't read
those Russian ones, either.

Siberia. I take it back—what could I conceivably know
about Siberia?

Didn't I say they were sitting right across from me? Because it was actually at a little angle from me that they were
sitting—since these were the days when a subway car on
the Lexington line had at one end two two-seater affairs
that were not exactly opposite one another but were sort
of off from each other at a little slant. Anyhow, the picture
I'm trying to get painted, it's them on one side and me on
the other and the rest of the car—believe it or not—this
is exceptional, I don't have to tell you—empty, empty, empty,
not one other fucking soul sitting or standing.

Can you beat it? From when they get on at Eighty-sixth
Street to when she got off without him at Forty-second,

there is nobody in this subway car but I and they. Or is it them and me?

Now *there* is the whole point of my telling you all of this in the first place, which is that *they*, the couple, didn't. I mean, get off the train in each other's company. And not only that, but *this*—which is that *he*, the Siberian fellow, he tricked her into it—actually faked her out, by hook and by crook got her onto the platform and then cut back into the car like a regular playmaker coming down the court without her.

No, I'm not doing this anywhere near right. I'm talking and I'm talking, but you do not know what the fuck is going *on*, and couldn't *possibly*.

I am starting again.

Here is the whole thing from the start again.

I said they got on at Eighty-sixth?

I get on at Eighty-sixth.

That is my practice—get on where I *have* to get on every workday morning—the Lexington line, the Broadway line, here, there, everywhere in the city. But what is instantly interesting the morning I am reporting on is that it is swept clean of people, the car that I get aboard on—except for them, of course—if they, the couple, *were* in fact already on it—the Siberians, the Thailanders, the Mongolians— you know, the whatever—huddled together in one of the two-seaters at one end of the car—a man and a woman— this is guesswork, of course—who I am guessing *must* be in their seventies at least—just little disks of faces to guess from, that's how hooded they were with scarves and caps

and weird coverings. So it is not just the eyes that give me
the Asian notion, not just the bones around the eyes, but
also the bandaged effect that gets imparted to the head when
these people are seeking ceremony or warmth. No, that's
off—that does not make any blessed sense.

Oh, Lord, I am really getting out of my depth with this.
It's just that you turn on the television and what do you
see but Tokyo, Seoul, whole columns of them shoulder-to-
shoulder, kids, endless legions of kids, always up in fucking
arms over this, that, or the other thing, their noggins all
done up with this ad-hoc crap on them, the whole street
chuggyjammed with them doing this slow, scary sort of creepy
Bangkokian jog shit.

So that's why I almost thought that, actually. Namely,
almost thought that they might both be Cong or Jap, except
that he was such a tall bugger, six-three, if I am any judge,
whereas she was a good one, too—the old woman, I mean—
every inch of her as tall as she had to be, and maybe then
some on top of it. Not that I ever was standing when either
of *them* was. Not that any of what I am saying to you is
anything but a guess. But you couldn't have thought about
it anymore than I was thinking about it, even saying to
myself, "Make up your mind," meaning, that I should make
up my mind what height was involved because I already
knew I might want to later on get some writing out of it—
a report, at least—and *now* look, that is just what I am
doing, aren't I, sitting there and getting debriefed?

But so what if she wasn't, and he wasn't, either? I mean,
even if the both of them put together weren't enough to

71

make up even one short human being, does that mean I have to go to bed without any supper?

It is not out of the question, the truth.

Wasn't there something somewhere in my reading, something I read somewhere where there is this region of the Orient where the people are positively tremendous?

But maybe I didn't read it. Maybe it was in a movie when it was raining and the whole school had to stay inside and couldn't have recess. You know, the climate and the crops and the trade routes of somewhere, and the enormous size of certain of its citizens. Or maybe we were doing a class project on cotton, and it was also the year of the adjective.

Which reminds me to tell you that I am not dumb. I promise you, I for one can speak to the distinction between that which is only morphologically adjectival and that which is instead syntactically thus.

Unless you forgot. I mean, about back there where I was giving the appearance of being flummoxed as to what you transmute Thailand to when you want to say, "I think that they both were . . ."

Wait. When you say, "The man was Mongolian," you replicate the morphology but not the function that is exhibited in "The man was a Mongolian."

But I imagine you have gone and forgotten all that. Ah, God, one offers speculations and, once offered, forgets.

Sorry.

Really.

Been farting around for altogether too long now. You've

got me dead to rights—just another man of action knocking his goddamn brains out to come across as a man of thought.

Meant *transform*, not *transmute*.

It's so hard.

You shouldn't have to know anything to do something. I mean, it doesn't seem fair, does it? But that's how the set-up is: know-how, smarts, skilled labor—fellows like me, nothing uncalled-for, nothing spontaneous. Ah, it's all such a lousy deal, start off with things which couldn't be simpler, and before you know it, what?

The answer is that you're struggling against great torrents of shit, complexities you never had the brains to create. Thought you were just doing arithmetic, yes? Whereas, Jesus, if you're not Boltzmann, you might as well be dead, be in your grave, be an idiot.

I saw them.

The car was empty.

I tell you, it was the coldest of damnable days! It was New *York* and I was freezing—and them, they—*they* looked so warm together—they looked like *Eskimos* together—the man and woman, they looked so *comfy* with each other, so *used* to things.

Assuming.

Because how much could I actually see of them?

You realize I am sitting in the seat that is almost exactly facing theirs? I mean, I had to. I had the whole car to choose from, sure—but let us not forget my specialty, my reason for being, why I was there, why I am here.

You'd look at me and see a fellow who doesn't look like anything—a big man in a big coat, lots of room for everything.

Oh, you bet, they could have been Eskimos.

They had to be something.

He kept scribbling things. He had in his pocket these folded-up papers and he kept getting them out and scribbling things on them—not words, of course, but numerals, I think, or symbols from sciences that we keep warning these people they have no fucking business messing with. Equations, disequilibriums, *things*. But, all right, this is not my element, and I would be the first to admit it.

On the other hand, just don't think I couldn't see him plain as day, the sonofabitch scratching away at these folded-up papers, the bastard acting as if he were up to something big—reaching for some extravagant result, putting on like some fucking Taiwani or something, some Taiwanese whizbang, some trafficker in new methodologies feeling his way by brainy frigging fingertip.

Oh, you know, you know—so absorbed he seemed, so utterly remote from things, the old broad meanwhile nattering away at him, all jabber, jabber, jabber without fucking let-up or surcease—get napkins, get ketchup, aren't we all out of mayo? Or so I was made to speculate—because *who* could fucking hear? And even if I could have, wouldn't it've been in Singaporese or something?

Or what is it, Singapo?

This is why you have to fill in. But I ask you, the blanks, whose fault is it that you have to fill them in?

Oh, yes, Dr. Wu, Dr. Wu—that's who's at the bottom of all of this, bigshot sitting over there and working out cosmological things in exponents of ten, Mrs. Wu going on at him and on at him, *get this, get that,* him not listening to the words but only to the music—all out of eggs, all out of bread, don't forget the eggs and the bread on your way home, Wen Lung!

I'll tell you the truth. It wasn't that many minutes between the time I got on and he got her to get off, but it was enough of them for me to make all of this up. You know, Dirac, Besso, Lorentz, and good old Wen Lung Wu, the dirty turncoat humping it on down to the U.N. with whatever he's got going on down there in the language of Hwei. Hey, and isn't that why the car is empty of other riders? Because a hit has been set up to cut the cocksucker off?

And doesn't Wennie know it, can't Wennie see for himself, can't the asshole put two and two together and get it that him and her have been marked for death? That they will never make it off this train in fewer than many pieces? That somewhere between here and Forty-second Street they are going to be gunned down, eradicated, interdicted, bumped the fuck off? Or maybe not until they get out and start running, screaming bloody-murder for the Secretary General to send the mounted fucking police and goddamn Swiss Guard to come save them, come save them, but really in fact digging the big picture, really in fact getting an honest and sincere feeling for how the odds went right the dickens down to zero the instant this third party had stepped on in here, the instant the big-coated motherfucker had got himself all aboard, confederates having cleared the car of all possible witnesses, confederates having closed off all possible prospects of escape, confederates having screwed down the hatches, confederates having, as it were, prepared all preparable matters, spot-cleaned the setting for the point-shooter, made way for our high-tech remover, heah come dee specialist wid dee Euher, and it going be seated with duh Thompson mute, so what is left for it but to put the best face on it and huddle, huddle close?

Ah, Christ, I hear her say, "Clorox, get Clorox, don't forget, make a note," and him, he writes $OQ^2 = t^2x^2 - y^2yz^2$ and thinks, "Goodbye, my love, goodbye, my love, goodbye."

But as I already told you, the old fraud faked her out at Forty-second. I mean, if he had meant to get rid of her, that's just what he did—got her off without him, got her good and off.

Oh, the old sly-sides!

I tell you, these people with their eyes, they are not for one instant to be trusted. Why, the rascal he leapt up with a great start as we drew into the station—fairly leapt, fairly leapt, I say—as if to say, "Good heavens, Mrs. Wu—your hubby appears to have been incalculably distracted—preoccupied beyond all fathoming—mercy sakes, dear lady, darned near made us miss our station—let us hasten, sweet wife, let us take ourselves away."

Oh, the dickens, the dirty dickens!

Imagine this. See it as I, your patriot, saw it—the old

reprobate flinging himself at the doors and she, the poor dear, staggering after—so completely bewildered, taken so completely unawares—plunging blindly after, bad on her ancient feet, I don't doubt, blisters galore, corns, spurs, calluses, great horny bunions—totally but totally disoriented, not to mention so dreadfully overcome by an absolute riot of agonies—but nevertheless making her way just well enough, gaining on her hubby just barely, while he, the fucking fourflusher, he executes the adroitest of pivots—and all with such gallantry, the very sheerest of chivalries, as in "Ladies first, ladies first, dearest lady of the realm."

Well, you know what I say? I say, "Radies first." *Radies, radies, radies*—her on the platform, him still with me on the train, the whole deal moving again, hell-bent for Thirty-third.

"Lealm." That's what the dirty prick said!

But to be absolutely evenhanded, I'll say this for him— which is that the rogue actually winked at me once the doors had closed and we were off and clattering along on our clangorous way again. By God, the bastard, he was sitting back down in the same seat when he let me have it—winked, like gunfire, just the once—pow! Then took out his folded-up papers, his little stub of a pencil, making, for my money, a great Jew-y show of the thing, the filthy fucking Chink.

Oh, let's not beat around the bush, the wag was *Writing Secret Stuff*—isn't it high time everybody just quit all the shit and said what he means?

But here's the thing, which *was* he, doing what he did—
dirty traitor or dirty savior?

Because you can see how it could go either way, answer
either claim.

At any rate, it was a local, as I said. Or if I didn't say
it, then I just did.

Forget it.

What we had to deal with there was its being Thirty-third
next. This means—go ahead and count them for yourself—
nine blocks to get the Euher out and get the Thompson on,
nine blocks to get the Thompson on and fire once, nine
blocks to fire once and get the Thompson off, nine blocks
to do what everybody is waiting for you to do and get everything back under your big, loose coat.

Adjectives—oh, *Christ*!

SPELL BEREAVEMENT

My sister says, "It's Daddy. It's about Daddy."

My mother gets on and says, "Don't cry. He will be all right. Please God in heaven, God is taking him into his loving embrace right this minute and the man will be all right."

My sister gets back on and says, "Daddy just went a little while ago. Daddy is gone."

My mother gets on and says, "I can't talk. Don't make me talk."

My sister gets back on and says, "So make up your mind, are you coming or not?"

My mother gets on and says, "No one could begin to tell you. You turn around and the man is gone."

My sister gets on and says, "We have to have your answer. So which is it, are you coming or not?"

My mother gets on and says, "Like that." My mother says, "Just like that." My mother says, "You couldn't believe it." My mother says, "I couldn't believe it." My mother says, "You blink an eye and that's that." My mother says, "Did you hear me, were you listening to me?" My mother says, "You blink an eye and it's goodbye and good luck."

My sister gets back on and says, "Now is when you have to decide. Not next year, not tomorrow, not after we hang up. Do you understand what I am saying to you? I am saying now, make up your mind right this minute now while we are talking to you because we do not have all day for you to wait around and decide."

My mother says, "There wasn't an instant when I didn't expect it, not for years was there a single instant when I didn't expect it. But you think it still didn't come to me as a surprise? I want you to know something—it came to me as a surprise. I can't breathe, that's how much it came to me as a surprise."

My sister gets on and says, "Do you realize we have to make plans? So what are we supposed to do if we don't know how to plan because we don't know if we're supposed to plan for you to come down or not?" My sister says, "Be reasonable for once in your life and tell me do we plan for you to come or do we go ahead and not make plans."

My mother says, "My head never once touched the pillow when I didn't expect to wake up with the unmentionable staring me right in the face." My mother says, "I want you to hear me say something—all of my life with that man I had to sleep with one eye open." My mother says, "Did you hear me say that? Did you hear what I said?" My mother says, "Please God that God is listening, because I as the man's wife never got a moment's rest."

My sister says, "Make up your mind. Are you making up your mind? Here, speak to Mother, tell Mother. Mother wants to know if your mind is made up."

My mother gets back on and says, "Talk to your sister, I can't talk."

My sister says, "So is it yes or is it no?"

My mother says, "The man was my husband. For going on sixty years next month, the man was my husband. So were you listening to what I said to you, almost sixty years next month?"

My sister says, "Is it the fare? You need us to help you with the fare?"

My mother says, "You don't have the money to come to your own father when he is dead?"

My sister gets on and says, "We have to make arrangements. We have to make calls."

My mother says, "Do you know what it costs to call from Miami to New York? Do you want me to tell you what it costs to call from Miami to New York? Do you think they give you free calls when someone is dead and you are calling from Miami to New York?"

My sister gets on and says, "Look, no one is saying that this isn't just as much of a blow to you as it is to us. But we can't just sit here and wait all day for you tell us what, if anything, you are going to decide to do. So once and for all, yes or no, you are coming or not?"

My mother gets back on and says, "Let me make one tiny little thing very clear to you—where there is a will, there is a way."

My sister says, "Let bygones be bygones—just say yes or just say no and whichever it is you feel you have to say, we give you our absolute assurance that we will do our very best to completely understand."

My mother says, "Talk to your sister. Try to make sense."

My sister says, "Don't tell me. Tell your mother. Your mother has a right to hear you express yourself as honestly as you can."

My mother says, "Take this, take this—I don't want to touch it—I can't even breathe yet, let alone pick up a telephone and talk."

My sister says, "You're making her sick. I already gave her a pill and now you are making her sick." My sister says, "I'm telling you, the woman has taken all she can take." My sister says, "If I could afford it, you know what?" My sister says, "If I had the wherewithal to do it, if I had the money lying around to do it, you know what?" My sister says, "I would run get a doctor for her even if I had to beg, borrow, or steal to do it for her because the woman should be given a good once-over by a good doctor, hopefully a specialist who is absolutely topnotch." My sister says, "But thank God the woman doesn't need it." My sister says, "Thank God the woman has the strength of a horse."

My mother says, "All his life the man was not a big moneymaker. But you know something? The man was good."

My sister says, "Let's be sensible. Let's bury the hatchet and work things out together. Do we plan for you to come down or do we not plan for you to come down? Give me a simple yes or no and we will know how to conduct our affairs after we have to hang up."

My mother says, "I am here to tell you, the man never made a fortune, but you cannot say the man was not too good for his own good."

My sister says, "I don't know how the woman is still standing on her feet. Don't torment her with this. Don't you know that you are tormenting her with this? Stop tormenting your mother."

My mother says, "The man was too good. But do they give you a medal for being too good? Listen to what I am telling you, your father was too good. The man was goodness itself. You know what your father was? Your father was too good for this world, this is what your father was."

My sister says, "I want you to know that I am getting ready to wash my hands of this." My sister says, "Do you want me to hang up?" My sister says, "Is that what you are waiting for, are you just sitting there waiting for us to hang up? Because if you want me to get off, believe me, I can get off."

My mother gets back on and says, "The man was a saint." She says, "Listen to what I said to you, did you hear what I said to you?" She says, "Ask anyone—a living saint."

My sister gets back on and says, "No one is saying this is easy for you. Do you think it is easy for me? But things do not get done without plans being made, and things have to get done within the next hour without fail." My sister says, "I have to make certain calls. People have to be called.

I am trying to call people and get things taken care of without causing Mother any undue excitement or any additional upset." My sister says, "Consider your mother's health. The woman is not young. The woman is totally devoid of any reserves of energy to draw from should, God forbid, worst come to worst. So don't make worst come to worst. Try to appreciate the fact that the woman is at her wit's end. The woman has not one more shred of energy left over for any more of your crap. So do I make myself clear? Or do I have to spell this out for you what I am saying to you when I say eighty-eight? Do I have to tell you what your mother has already been through today and she only just an hour ago woke up? So are we going to get your answer or are we going to have to scream ourselves hoarse? Because all your mother wants to know is if she and I are supposed to expect you to come down here or if we are not. So are we or aren't we? Or is it your instructions to us that we are to go ahead and plan your own father's memorial service without his beloved son? Is that what your instructions are?"

My mother says, "You don't have to do me any favors. You do not have to do anybody any favors. Do as you please. If you want to come, come—if you don't want to come, don't come—the world will go on very nicely with or without you. Your father does not require your presence if it is too big a bother for you to come to him when he really needs you to be here in attendance."

My sister gets back on and says, "Is he listening to us?"

My mother says, "It is not a necessity. There is no necessity. If you can't make it, you can't make it. Not everybody in the world can always be expected to just drop everything and run. I promise you, it is no disrespect if you couldn't make it. No one would accuse you of nothing. Your father would not accuse you of nothing. Your father would be the first person to tell you to do what you have to do if it is a question of prior business making a prior claim on you which couldn't be avoided at any cost. If it's business, don't give it a second thought. So which is it, business or not business? Because if it is business, then it's all well and good. Believe me, your father would be the first one to go along with the fact that not everybody has a situation where they can afford just at the drop of a hat to take time off from their business, come rain or come shine."

My sister says, "If it's the money, then maybe Mother can get you something out of savings and reimburse you when you get down here for whatever you had to lay out for it out of your own pocket. So talk to Mother, tell her what your situation is, tell her what you have in mind, make a clean breast of it and get it out on the table with her and I am sure a solution can be found and it will all work out. But if all it is is the ticket down and the ticket back, you could see who maybe has a special on right now for night flights if you left sometime tonight. So why don't you maybe call up around town and get the best price and then call us right back?"

My mother gets back on and says, "The man only wanted

the best for his family." My mother says, "The man's every waking thought was for no one but his family." My mother says, "The man could never do enough for his family." My mother says, "The man never wanted one thing for anyone but his family." My mother says, "His family's happiness, this alone is what made the man happy." My mother says, "Wait a minute—*not* his family's happiness, but *your* happiness—yours, *you*, the professor, the *poet*, the boy, his darling, his son."

My sister says, "This has gone on long enough. I am not asking again. Yes or no? Either answer the question or forget about it, because I am hanging up."

My mother says, "It is no crime if you cannot come. No one is going to say that there should be a finger pointed at you if you cannot come. You come or you do not come, you only have to suit yourself."

My sister gets back on and says, "Don't kid yourself, it is a crime, it is a sin, it makes me sick to be his sister."

My mother gets back on and says, "I am just trying to think what would make the most sense for all parties concerned."

My sister gets back on and says, "Drop dead. He should do everybody a favor and drop dead. Did you hear what I said to you? He makes me sick."

My mother gets back on and says, "Be nice. Don't fight."

My sister says, "I am giving you one more chance." My sister says, "Do you want another chance?" My sister says, "As God is my witness, this is your last chance."

My mother says, "He's listening, he's listening." My mother says, "Don't worry, he's listening." My mother says, "Talk turkey to him, tell him what the situation is."

My sister says, "Your mother wants to hear your voice. Try to act like a human being. Let the woman hear your voice."

My mother says, "Talk to me, darling. I am listening, darling. Let me hear my darling talk."

My sister says, "Let him go ahead and drop dead. Stop begging him. Stop babying him. Stop pampering him. You know what would serve him right? If he hung up the phone and dropped dead."

My mother says to me, "Your father loved you like life itself." My mother says to me, "You know what your mother is saying to you when she says to you like life itself?"

My mother says to me, "Speak to me, sweetheart."

My mother says to me, "Talk to me, sweetheart."

My mother says to me, "Tell your mother what it is which is in her darling's heart of hearts."

What is in my heart of hearts?

There are not people in my heart of hearts.

There are just sentences in my heart of hearts.

So what was I to say to them?

Not to the locutions of discourse but to my mother and my sister.

Because I really honestly do not think that there was any

way for me to say to them why I was not answering what
they said. I mean, let's not be ridiculous. You can't just
turn around and say to people—good God, to your own
most beloved loved ones—that you are too disabled to talk
because what you are doing is meanwhile going crazy with
pencil and paper so as not to miss one word.

THE PROBLEM OF
THE PREFACE

This is a story about a man who was done in by a story, and by that, by done in, it is meant killed—killed in the very realest sense. It is a very straightforward affair from its start to its finish, the only question being this—is it, was it, made up? Oh, but no, no, no—the question is not whether this story is made up, but whether that one was, that one being the one that our hero was done in by, for it was— and here is the nastiest spicule in the whole sorry business— a story that he himself was the one who told.

And had he not?

But tell it he did, and over and over.

As we ourselves shall have now to do, to offer—wouldn't you know it?—the effect of truth.

Behold.

This is the story the dead fellow told.

He said that jelly apples were coming around and that he ran to his father to get the money for one and that no sooner did he have the jelly apple and did bite of it than, lo, he set to choking to death upon it, but along came his brother who happened to notice and who got him by the belt and who hiked him up and who turned him over and who held him upside-down and who shook him good and proper, such that what had got itself stuck down inside of him came right up and fell out of him, and then there, by heaven, he was, restored to himself and right as any rain and thus a creature who was adoring forever everlastingly of his brother, never mind this latter's fate.

Or maybe he'd change his tune and tell it like this, say somebody was coming with jelly apples, so he went and told his father about it and his father said there was always going to be somebody who was going to be coming with something, that if they weren't coming with one thing, then they were going to be coming with another thing, that there wasn't anything which they were ever going to be coming with which was not going to cost somebody some money, but that the father wasn't a father ever to deny any son something, least of all mere wisdom and some candied nutrition.

But it all worked out to be the same story, anyway—one bite and the boy was choking to death on whatever he had bitten into—take your pick, jelly apple, sourball, peanut. Whereupon, here comes his brother to come happening along and thereupon to see what has been going on, so that he takes the boy by the belt and yanks him up and turns him over and holds him upside-down, et cetera, et cetera, until the piece of whatever it was gets knocked loose and comes back up out of him and he is breathing all right again and feels altogether returned to himself again, just like a full-fledged brought-back-from-the-dead person, even if the whole deal is fake.

This is the story the dead man told.
Or *that* was.

Now, as to how it got him killed?
The answer could never be simpler.
The storyteller told the story to his son—who just could not wait to grow up enough to get strong enough to do the same thing which had been so robustly extolled of, who just could not wait to be ready enough for the chance when his father started choking enough, which eventually—as will any of us—the father regrettably, but not all that excessively, did.
Oh boy oh boy oh boy!
From the son's point of view, it was all for love, whereas from the viewpoint of the father, death was no more than the cost of the narrative endeavor paid out to the end of its course. Yet whichever adornment you choose to decorate the natural irony of the text with, the fact is that the kid managed to get the old man head over heels, all right, but that after upending him, the old rascal slipped away for an instant and cracked something pretty critical, a stiletto of neck-bone thence—*oh, shit!*—nicking its way up into the back of a drastically literal brain.

LEOPARD IN A TEMPLE

Look, let's make it short and sweet. Who anymore doesn't go crazy from overtures, from fanfares, from set-ups, from preambles, from preliminaries? So, okay, here is the thing—this is my Kafka story, fine and dandy. Actually, it is going to be my against-Kafka story. Because what I notice is you have to have a Kafka story one way or the other. So this is my Kafka story, only it is going to be one which is against Kafka. Which is different from being against Kafka's *stories*, although I would probably be against those, too, if I ever went back and really reread any of them.

I'm not interested.

It's exclusively the man himself which I am interested in.

But not to the extent that I would give you two cents for him even if he was made of money, which is what I understand the man in his lifetime was.

I'll tell you about lifetimes.

I have a person here who is a kindergartner, so right

there that takes care of lifetimes. Whereas I don't have to tell you that what Kafka got was *nafkelehs*.

You say this Kafka knew a lot. But show me where it says he knew from doily-cutters.

Or even what cutters were who didn't work in paper.

Take my dad, for a convenient comparison.

The man couldn't make a go of it in business.

In other words, so far as his fortunes went, if dry goods was hot, then he was in wet ones.

But who has the energy for so much history?

Kafka, on the other hand, the man doesn't even know the meaning of the word idle, that's how fast he sits himself down to write his own father a letter. But let me ask you something? You want to read to me from the book where it says he ever had the gall to also jump out and say boo to his mother?

Save your breath.

I am not uninformed as to the character of the author.

Pay attention—we are talking about a creature who could not wait to stab the son of a butcher in the back—but where is it on exhibit that this Kafka Schmafka ever had the belly to split an infinitive?

Now take me and my mother, to give you two horses of a totally different color.

You know what?

We neither of us ever had one.

Or even a rented pony.

You see what I am saying to you? Because I am saying to you that nothing is out-of-bounds so far as I myself am personally concerned—unless it is something which is so dead and buried that I have got nothing to gain from unearthing it, which she, the old horseless thing, doesn't happen to be yet.

But Kafka, so how come wherever you turn, it's Kafka, Kafka—just because brushing his own teeth, the man couldn't help himself, the toothbrush alone could make him vomit?

You know what I say?

I say this Kafka had it too good already, a citizen in good standing in the Kingdom of Bohemia, whereas guess who gets to live out his unpony-ed life in the United States of unprincely America?

In a mixed building.

In even an apartment which is mixed also.

With a kindergartner—who is meanwhile, by the way, looking to me not just like the bug he looked to me like when he came into this world but also more and more like he is turning into a person who could turn big and normal and dangerous.

You want to hear something?

In kindergarten, they teach reading already. So the teacher makes them make a doily and then lay it down over some Kafka and recite through the holes to her.

This day and age!

These modern times!

Listen, I also woke up in my room once, and guess what.

Because the answer is I was still no different.

From head to toe, I had to look at every inch of what I took to bed with me.

95

Hey, you want to hear something?

I was *un*metamorphosed!

You look like I look, you think you get a Felice? Because the answer is that you do not even get a Phyllis.

FEE-LEE-CHAY.

"Oh, Feeleechay, my ancestor is a swine, a philistine, a businessman, a barbarian—so quick, quick, if you're for art and beauty, touch my dick!"

But to be fair, my mother used to say KLEE-YON-TELL.

Still does, I bet.

You know what I bet? I bet if I ever could get my mother on the telephone, you know what she would say to me? The woman would say to me, "Sweetheart, you should come down here to visit me down here, because they cater down here to the finest kleeyontell."

One time I went to call her up once, but never did it, never did.

Had to scream bloody-murder instead.

Hate to admit it, but I did.

Didn't do anything but that, didn't do anything but howl.

From flipping around the Rolodex cards and then seeing what was on her card when the cards fell open to hers.

You know what I say?

Who wishes the man ill? But I would like to see him wake up to what I wake up to.

Just once.

Forget it.

The man was small potatoes.

My dad lived through fifty years as a cutter in girls' coats, whereas Kafka, the pansy, could not even shape up and live through his own life.

But why argue?

Where's the sense?

It wasn't a cockroach on my mother's card. It was just a half-asleep earwig instead.

THE HILT

Oh, the pleasure Solovei took in the manner of Shea's death, never mind that it was a suicide and Shea the very paradigm of what Solovei could not but help but helplessly think of whenever he, Solovei, had thought to set himself the meditation of what it must be to be the Gentile—oh so very big-boned, large-boned, heavy-boned, long and broad in all the central categories, the blithe inventor of every wreckless declension, the very thing of this vexing life most lived.

And never mind that Solovei loved Shea.

Solovei loved Shea's death more.

Could not keep himself from telling everyone:

"You hear about poor Shea? Jesus, the man drove himself off a fucking cliff. Took his car out and went poking up along the coast and found himself what looked to him to be the very spot which was high enough and then sailed the sonofabitch right off."

Or so the story went.

The story that had been carried cross-country to Solovei

by those who had still been keeping company with Shea right up until Shea's very end.

Not that Solovei and Shea had ever had a falling out. Just that Solovei had come to arrive at a time in his life when it was more and more seeming to him to be necessary for him to keep himself more and more to his own small experience. This is why when Solovei told everyone about poor Shea, it was via the telephone that Solovei would pass along the news.

It made him ashamed.

"Hello?"

"Hi, this is Solovei."

"I'm calling about Shea."

"You remember, my old buddy Shea—big guy? Great big happy bastard, great big cheerful happy chap, with sort of what you might call indomitably red hair?"

"Anyway, I just got this call from California and you'll never guess."

It seemed to Solovei nothing short of a veritable show of heroics in himself that he could keep telephoning the word around when here it kept making the fellow feel so horribly ashamed of himself to be doing it.

"Ah, God, the bravery it must have taken in him to have actually taken hold of that goddamn wheel."

And so saying, have a vision of the hands of his friend Shea—great hams of hands, as Solovei understood these Gentiles to say.

Meaty.

Big-freckled.

Letting go and gripping elsewise and then yanking your mind that long, clattering, blazing, disastrous way.

Jesus Christ.

The fucking courage of Shea!

To which she said, "Oh, it is certainly not a question of living or of dying but only of the hilt."

Solovei did not get this.

He said, "Hilt?"

She said, "Why it has got its teeth so fiercely into you like this, Shea's doing away with himself—the fact that, like his life, how he did it was right up to the hilt."

"Oh," Solovei said.

"Yes, of course," Solovei said.

"Sure," Solovei said.

"Yes, I suppose so," Solovei said.

And knew that his interlocutor had uncovered the truth.

She.

Her.

One of the ones Solovei had stopped feeling the necessity of keeping up with when he had started feeling the necessity of keeping closer to himself.

"Come on over and we'll fuck," she said.

"You're spooked," she said.

"It'll get you unspooked," she said.

"Come fuck," she said.

"Maybe sometime soon," Solovei said, and then, with real terror in his heart, hung up.

.   .   .

As for what is left of the story, Solovei never did go to have his little visit with her but did have, some months thereafterward, a dream in which he had in fact set out to have it, the visit, and in it saw himself in his car motoring along the highway to her house, whereupon suddenly also saw—that is, the Solovei sleeping saw the Solovei driving— himself having to perform an amazing sequence of un-imaginably shrewd maneuvers to elude the enormous truck that had abruptly been revealed bearing so brutally down upon him from his blind side, which was both of his sides.

In his dream, Solovei could even hear himself already telephoning all of the friends he used to have.

"Hi."

"It's me."

"It's Solovei."

"I was on my way over to see Shea's old wife."

"I had the car out, just to pay a condolence call, I couldn't have conceivably have been driving more cautiously, when out of the fucking blue there is all of a sudden right out of nowhere alongside of me this gigantic fucking truck.

"Anyway, it's a miracle, the stunts I could all of a sudden so incredibly do with that wheel and those brakes and my mind."

MY TRUE STORY

Myrna, Linda, Lily, Janice, Shirley, Rhonda, Barbie, Bar-
bara, Sylvia, Marilyn, Elaine, Georgia, Iris, Natalie, Patty,
Joyce, Binnie, Robin, Molly, Mrs. Shea, Lucille, Marie,
Maria, Valerie, Barbara, Grace, Stephanie, Caroline,
Tina, Eliza, Edwina, Evelyn, Edna, Joanna, Jeanne,
Janet, Enid, Edith, Laurella, Lorrie, Lorraine, Myra, Emily,
Kate, Cathy, Constance, Hedy, Heidi, Barbara, Katrina,
Denise, Josephina, Rosalind, Roberta, Leslie, Lettie, Bar-
bara, Geraldine, Theodora, Patricia, Lena, Lena's sister,
Felicia, Emmie, Effie, Ellie, Nettie, Nancy, Blissie, Nell,
Nellie, Lilly, Nora, Barbara, Lillian, Helen, Helene, Mrs.
Rose, Joy, Ann, Nan, Jan, Deb, Sue, Barbie, Susannah,
Suzanne, Mary, Barbara, Barbara, Barbara, Martha, Sheila,
Sheilah, Deirdre, Barbara, Cynthia, Cindy, Belle, Betty,
Belinda, Bertha, Bettina, Barbie, Betsy, Blossom, Brenda,
Brigette, Bronwen, Bessie, Barbara, Barbara, Barbie, Bar-
bara, Barbara, Barbara.

There have been buckets more than those, of course.

But it would be indecent for me to list beyond the last name listed. It is sufficient to say that I proved to exhibit an exorbitant fondness for the name Barbara and finally offered marriage to a person whose name was thus.

She accepted.

We were wed.

I have lived blissfully ever since.

O, Bliss!

I have been joyful ever since.

O, Joy!

This heart is pure and overflowing.

O, Accepta!

O, Wedda!

O, hoshana in the highest!

Hoshana?

BALZANO & SON

I expect that it is necessary for me to tell you the true story of my father's shoes—for I have so often told—if not you, then others—such false stories of my father's shoes, sometimes claiming for my father's shoes some sort of formal irregularity that would enforce the thought of there being a certain abnormality of the feet my father had.

But there was nothing exceptional about my father's feet. My father's feet were perfectly routine feet. My own feet seem to me no different from my father's feet, and my feet—can I not see my feet?—are entirely routine.

Ah, but here I am, already cheating.

I mean, it is shoes, my father's shoes, that I have been inviting you to prepare yourself to hear me tell the truth of, not the feet my father put into his shoes.

The firm of Balzano & Son made them, made all of them, dozens of them for each of the four seasons, all with the maker's mark worked somewhere into the buttery lining of each shoe's interior, Balzano & Son in the left shoe, Balzano

& Son in the right shoe, and for each Balzano & Son shoe
there would be a bespoke Balzano & Son shoetree—I believe my father called them something else but I do not
recall what my father called them, these lacquered shoetrees
in woods better than your chairs—formed to fit that exact
shoe exactly, and it too, that shoetree too, declaring that
it would also like to argue for the theory of its provenance,
the name Balzano & Son incised into the good wood of each
shoetree, the left one and the right.

But where is the truth in any of this?

I cannot prove that Balzano and his son were not liars.

Who is to say what Balzano's name was before it was
Balzano? And the son, what of him? Great Jesus, how can
one ever know if the fellow was not adopted?

Fellow!

Why fellow?

How fellow?

This Balzano, could not the rascal have elected to change
a gender or make an offspring up!

No, I cannot tell you the true story of my father's shoes.
I withdraw the statement of my ambition to do so. It was
foolish to have admitted to such a program. Such a program
is not possible. Indeed, it may even be that I cannot tell
you a true story of any object exterior to my own person,
save to remark that when he succumbed—I mean, of course,
my father—I came to have his wristwatch and that it is an
Audemars Piguet wristwatch and that it is said to be pos-
sessed of the properties to fetch—appraiser after appraiser

so stated to me when I took the thing around to them to make my aggrieved inquiries—just shy of $10,000.

Oh, but no again!

I just thought of something.

With respect to my father's shoes, it just this instant occurred to me that there is a little tale I might disclose to you and which could have the look of reliability enough.

This:

That I would take a cloth to my father's shoe closet to rub the dust off of them, to show the sign of my devotion to him, one so often doing so because one so certainly knew one's father to be so devoted to them oh so very much, and quite understandably so, quite so absolutely understandably so, such quality of leathers, such character of the maker's craft.

After school and before he came home.

Undoing all of the laces to a depth of two sets of eyelets so as to enhance my labor's not going without the small prospect of being at least a little noticed.

It exhausted me, and it exhausted it—the playtime of my boyhood—this activity of my youth.

Hours, so many hours, it does not please me that I lost them.

So do not ask me what time it is. He is dead and I am his son—and am succeeding in refuting the truth of truth.

THE FRIEND

I live in a big building and my son lives in a big building, so I meet all kinds and I hear what I hear. And why not, why shouldn't I listen? I am a person with such an interesting life he couldn't afford to be interested in someone else's? They talk, I pay attention—even if when they are all finished I sometimes have to say to myself, "The deaf don't know how good they got it. The deaf got no complaint coming."

Take years ago, this lady—we are biding our time down there in my boy's place, the room in the basement they got set aside for the convenience of the laundry of tenants.

Some convenience.

Who is a tenant?

I am not a tenant.

This lady is not a tenant.

What is the case here is our *children* are the tenants—my boy, her girl—and *theirs* are the things which are in the washing machines and in the dryers and why I and the lady in question are sitting in a terrible dirtiness waiting. So P S, it's two total strangers twiddling their thumbs in a room in a basement down underneath a very big building, when what you hear from one of these people—not from me but from her, from this woman I just mentioned—is a noise like she wants you to think it's her last.

You know. You have heard. It is the one which, give us time, we all hear—because who doesn't, just give yourself time, in the long run finally make it?

So I naturally say to the woman, "What? What?" And the woman says to me, "You don't want to know."

That's it for the preliminaries.

Here is what comes next.

She says, "You—you got a son—don't worry, I know, I know—and don't think I don't also know what you are going through, either—because I know—I got eyes—I see, I know—you don't have to tell me anything—you don't have to breathe one word—I got eyes in my head to see for myself, thank you—no one has to tell me what the score is—believe me, your heartache is your own affair—but just so you know I know—with him you got plenty, you got all anyone should ever have to handle—but just count your lucky blessings—because I got worse—there is worse in the world than a window-dresser for a son—there is worse than a delicate child—sure, sure, don't tell me, I heard, I heard—and don't think my heart don't go out to you, bad as I got plenty worse of my own—a daughter, not a son—a daughter—Doris—Deedee—forty-odd and still all alone in the world—and for why, for why—not that someone is claiming the girl is any Venus de Milo—but so who is, who is—and is this the be-all and end-all, to be so gorgeous they all come running—believe me, she is some catch for the right boy— for a boy which knows which end is up, this is a girl which is a catch and a half for such a boy—but shy—a shyness like this you could not even fathom—a shyness like this, who knows how it develops—even to me, the mother, it is a total mystery, I can tell you—so a rash, a rash—like a dryness even, like not even a rash but just a dryness—the skin here—the cheeks—so like it is not exactly appetizing to look at her at certain periods of the season, if you know what I am saying to you—so what is this—is this the end of the world, is this the worst tragedy I could cite to you, a little dryness the child could always rub something into and who would notice—but skip it—the girl is mortified— the girl is humiliated—the girl is total mortification itself— because in Deedee's eyes, forget it, this is all there is, in the whole wide world there is nothing else but her complexion, her skin—so it flakes, so it sheds a little, so for this life should come to a halt—you don't give them a special invitation, does anyone notice—no one notices—who cares— no one cares—no one even sees—dry skin, you think people don't look and see character first—first, last, and always what they see is what is a person's worth—but who can tell her—who can reason—it is nothing, absolutely nothing, the very mildest of conditions—but for Deedee forget it— for her it is curtains—that shy, that bashful, ashamed of her own shadow—so could you get her to be a little social—

111

you couldn't get her to budge for nothing—God forbid someone should have eyes in his head—a little nothing here—where I am showing you—makeup would cover it over so who could even guess—but does this please her—nothing pleases her—her own company pleases her—a movie every other week, this is for Deedee a very satisfying experience—but for me, if you want to know, from just when I think about it, alone for all her life, I could cut my throat from ear to ear—forget boyfriend—does the girl have a friend even—because the girl has nothing—the girl has her complexion to look at—forget a nice decent marriage to a nice decent boy—and just to add insult to injury, what with so many of them deciding to be boys like yours, where even are the high hopes anymore—but meanwhile is it too much to ask that for my Doris there should be at least a companion to travel the road of life with—because, I ask you, doesn't everybody have a right to somebody—but her, she wouldn't even go out looking, God forbid somebody should see a little redness, a little dryness, some peeling where if she only used a good moisturizer on herself and did it on a regular basis with some serious conscientiousness, I promise you, the whole condition would vanish quicker than you could snap your little finger—but her—her—who can talk to her—my Deedee—my Doris—God love her—but just thank God that at her office it is a different story entirely—just thank God that at her place of business they couldn't get enough of her—always Doris this and Doris that—I am telling you, they are devoted to the girl—devoted—what they wouldn't do for her—like you wouldn't believe it, but

just this last Christmas they sent her off for seven days
gratis—not one red penny did the girl have to reach into
her own pocket for—the whole arrangement was bought
and paid for—the whole arrangement was signed, sealed,
and delivered—and not Atlantic City neither but Acapulco—Acapulco—this is how indispensable to these people
the girl happens to be—all expenses paid—every red nickel—
first-class from start to finish—the best—bar none—so when
I heard this, I said to myself, 'God willing, she'll get away,
it'll be a change of pace, a change of scenery, et cetera, et
cetera—and who knows but that maybe a little romantic
interlude is just around the corner—after all, a nice resort,
a nice hotel, these Latin fellows, whatever'—but now I have
to laugh—you heard me—laugh—because you think she
didn't come back worse than when she went—go think again—
this is why I am here where you see me right now—this is
why I have to be here to do for her and do for her—the
wash, the cleaning, the shopping, whatever—with my legs,
twice a week, from Astoria, I have to come in all the way
on my feet from Astoria—but thank God the girl has a
mother who can still wait on her hand and foot—because
thanks to Acapulco, look who's got on her hands a nervous
wreck for a daughter—you heard me, a total bundle of
nerves—but totally—but utterly—say boo to the girl, she
jumps from here to there—and you know what—I don't
blame her—you wouldn't neither—when you hear what
you will hear, believe me, you wouldn't believe it—upstairs
up there in her apartment there and just sits around all
the time listless, no color in her face, a figment of her former

self—would she go outside for just some air—goes to the bathroom and that's it—who even knows if she goes when I am not here—me—coming in all the way from Astoria— with legs like these—if you could believe it, twice a week."

The woman gives me on the knee like a tap with her fingers and then she picks herself up and with another groan again she goes and checks on the things she put for her daughter in the machine, whereupon the woman then turns herself around and says to me, she says, "Your boy, tell me, you got just the one son?" But why should she wait for an answer? I promise you, people know there is something which whenever you look at a father's face, you don't need to ask another question. "Sure, sure," she says, sticks in two more quarters in her dryer, and comes back to where she was in the first place and then plunks herself down with another new groan in the row of chained-down chairs.

She says, "Pardon me, but do I still have your undivided attention? Because I know you got your mind on your own kid and your own troubles but you didn't hear yet what happened, which is that the child goes down there and it couldn't be more perfect—the weather, the service, the accommodations—everything is absolutely first-class, so all she has to do is jump into a bathing suit and start being the happiest girl in the whole wide world. But does she go sit around the pool like the other youngsters do, so that maybe there might arise a little excitement from whichever direction? The answer is no, the girl didn't even begin to. Instead, she drags herself all the way out to the beach with the wind and the sand, which is utterly unnecessary, and with a book and not even a little bag with at least a lipstick in it, she knocks herself out finding herself a place as far away from everybody else in the world as is humanly possible and, lo and behold, this is how the girl spends the five days, the six days, whatever you actually get when they give you a week's free vacation, and not once, when all is said and done, not once does the girl have a single solitary conversation with a person of any gender. She reads a book, and this is the entire nature of her entertainment, period, with the lone sole exception of this friend she makes, this little animal which comes running along the beach to her and comes up to her, like she thinks a little Mexican hairless or whatnot, like this tiny little dog like the bandleader, like this Xavier Cugat, if you remember, used to hide in his pockets, a Chihuahua is what they call it, two Chihuahuas, a different Chihuahua in each pocket. So the whole first day, would the thing go away? Forget it, what it loves in this world is all of a sudden my unmarried daughter, it couldn't get enough of my own personal daughter, huggy-huggy, kissy-kissy, two permanent lovebirds from the first minute they laid eyes on each other. So naturally the next day the girl can't wait to get back out to the beach again, God forbid her friend should miss her for two minutes, and this time she's got with her what? Because the answer is a handbag. Do you hear this, a handbag! But for lipstick and mascara and eye shadow? Don't make me laugh. Because the answer is it's not for something serious but instead so she can sneak her brand-new one-and-only in through the

115

lobby and up in the elevator and for the rest of the whole vacation feed it scraps from the table and watch it sleep between two clean sheets in the bed with her like a person, please God it shouldn't have its little head on the pillow. And why not? In all the girl's whole life, aside from her mother, who ever paid her two seconds' worth of attention before? But on the other hand, outside of her mother, tell me who ever got the chance. Even the girl's own father, may the man rest in peace, had to hire an army every time he wanted the child to hold still so he could talk to her or get even a good look at her in the light.

"So next comes the terrible crisis. Are you listening? Because time's up and now you have to gather yourself together and pack your luggage and face the facts that you threw away your one big chance and say so long to paradise. But could the girl even begin to tear herself away from the first real friend she ever in all her born days had? This thing, could the child just say to it that's it and that's it, now goodbye and good luck?

"Don't hold your breath.

"Weeks later, when she could open up her mouth to even first begin to speak again, the child actually said to me, 'Mother, I think I would have eaten poison before I could have left it behind. *Poison.*'

"Poison, some joke. Believe me, when you hear what's coming, you'll say to yourself the same as me, ha ha, poison, that's a good one, some laugh, poison.

"So don't ask me why, but this is how determined the

girl is, because even with all of the reasons you couldn't in a million years get away with it, the answer is she *did*. All the way back to New York, right past all of the bigshots with their badges and their everything, and then right out of the airport past the customs and the rest of it, and then right here into this same building where, God love him, I know he's got his own problems too, your own lifelong heartache, your boy, with all of his gorgeous costumes and his window-dressing, also rents a nice dwelling—from Acapulco to New York, here comes my Deedee with her one-and-only.

"But as soon as it gets here, would it eat? Could she get it to do anything but drink water? Maybe the airplane ride gave it an upset stomach, who knows—meanwhile all it wants is water and to lay around and vomit, and it wouldn't even touch a single morsel or have the strength to play with her or even let her kiss it. So by now the girl is thoroughly beside herself with panic—she is so frantic the child cannot even see straight—so what does she do but pick the thing up and wrap it up in a towel because it is cold out and God forbid her adorable darling should catch a chill and get any worse—and then she runs out into the street with it—like a crazy woman to go find the dog-and-cat doctor which is up the block from here—on the other side—after you pass the big Shopwell in the middle of the block.

"God bless him, the man can see with his own two eyes that the girl is positively hysterical—so he quick puts everything to one side and takes her right in—and he says to her, 'Sit, wait,' he'll be right back with his diagnosis, first he's got to get out his instruments and examine—and meanwhile the child is shrieking, 'Don't hurt him, don't hurt him!' "

The woman looks at me and she says to me, "So did you hear me with both ears—*instruments, examine—don't hurt him, don't hurt him?*"

She gives her chest a grab like there is gas inside of it, and she says to me, "Go check your machine—there's time yet—with children like ours, where are we running?"

You think I don't know a storyteller like this one? I promise you, in this department, I myself was not exactly born yesterday, these people with all of their teasings and their winks and their punch lines. But by the same token, who wanted to offend such a person? Because, for one thing, you never know when you might require the company, and meanwhile let us not forget who else of my acquaintance also makes his residence in the very building and could always use a friendly neighbor's mother with an open-minded opinion. So this I can give you every assurance of, I myself did not intend to burn up any bridges behind me.

This is why I got up and felt inside of the dryer—even though I didn't even have to actually touch anything to see that they all had a little way still to go yet. And then, like a perfect gentleman, I come back and I sit down and I signify to the woman that I am all ears and at her beck and call whenever she is ready to please continue. But strictly between you and me, so far as punch lines go, in all of history they never invented a second one.

She says, "Two seconds." She says, "The man is in there all of two seconds with his examining." She says, "The man comes out with his white coat and his rubber gloves and he says to the child, he says, 'Darling, I am afraid that I must inform you that your pet has a mild case of rabies—you didn't get near any of his saliva, did you?'

" 'Oh, God, God!' my daughter screams, and then it dawns on my Deedee, *rabies*, and she shrieks, 'No, I'm fine, I'm fine—just give me back my dog, I want to get a second opinion, I want to see another doctor!'

"So what does this one say to that?

"Mister, are you listening to me when I ask you what this one says to that? Because here is the answer the whole wide world has been waiting for. Which is that the man, the doctor, the specialist gives the girl a look and he says very calmly to her, '*Dog*? That animal in there is no *dog*, lady. What you brought in here is a rat.' "

You know something? Because I am telling you the truth when I tell you this. For some crazy reason, after I heard what I heard, I did not know what the next thing to do was. I mean, my son's clothes, I did not know if I could bear to touch them anymore—not even when I knew that if I went to get them, they would be as clean and as dry as a bone.

AGONY

In that case, there were two men and a woman. The photographer may also have been a woman, to go with one of
the men. But I never looked to see. I only watched the
others, the three who were getting ready, their backs to me.

Perhaps their span hid the fourth party, the one with
the camera.

I think of that now, thinking why I did not notice the
photographer, since the persons getting ready faced away
from me and, therefore, I faced the fourth party.

I cannot say what the three of them looked like—except
that the men were husky by my standard, wide-waisted,
one man considerably the taller of the two. And there was
this: the woman had no appeal that I could see.

My attention was mainly elsewhere. It was captured by
the placement of the arms of these people as they prepared
themselves for the picture, the woman between the men,
the men reaching behind her to rest a hand on each other's
shoulder, the woman with both arms out, to hold each man

from behind, her fingers taking them tight by the waist—
wide waists, as I remember it.

They all hugged like that when they were ready.

Then they dropped their arms, and you knew, without
looking, that the picture had been taken.

I saw them stand there for a while, facing away from me,
all three, the two men and the woman, arms at their sides—
each of those three with his arms down then.

I remember something else now.

One of the men—the shorter, I think—wore very bright
corduroy trousers, very bright green, and a pale yellow
sweater.

Then they had their arms up in place again, in approx-
imately the same places.

They were getting ready again.

They hugged. I could tell they were hugging hard.

Then they put their arms down, lowered them swiftly to
their sides—and I knew another picture had been made.

That was the end of the picture-taking.

My son was with me that day. It was a day for us in the
park.

He was riding his bicycle and I was there to watch him
do it. But for the time I watched the picture-taking, I was
not watching my son ride.

But when I started watching him again, he was riding
very well—and even doing some tricks.

I called to him. I said, "Come over here a minute!" and

when he rode up to me, he said, "How did you like that?"

I said, "I've got a good idea."

He said, "Did you like the way I did that?"

I said, "Let's go home and get the camera and then we'll come back here and I'll take a picture of you on your bike."

He said, "What do you think of what I did? I was pretty great, wasn't I?"

I said, "Let's go home and get the camera."

We did that.

We went home. But we never got the camera to go take the picture in the park.

Something came up. I don't remember what. But something did.

I'm sorry that happened, but another day will come. I expect we will get to it, the picture, before the weather turns too cold.

My plan is to produce a photograph of my son on his bicycle. I am very proud of him, of how skillfully he rides the thing—and, of course, you may have guessed from this how I love him very much.

My plan is to have the camera with me the next time we go. My plan is to find somebody and show him how the camera works. It's a very simple camera.

I'll hand it over and stand behind my son.

The way I see it, the bicycle will be positioned broadside to the camera, my son sitting on the seat, in an attitude of motion and of happiness perhaps. I will be standing just behind him, my arm holding him across the shoulders, that or some other such gesture to exhibit that I am touching him and keeping him from falling over.

And then we will be like that until the picture-taking is over.

DON'T DIE

My facts are not unknown. This notwithstanding, mine is a history which has never been without its share of detractors. But I feel, however, that we can safely say the truth must speak for itself. For example, the period of incarceration was not excessive. As an institution, it was viewed in the highest regard. Each and every member of the staff was of a generously professional caliber. I am not claiming to the contrary, or asserting in any fashion, that there might not have been the infrequent individual incorporated here and there who would not in every respect pass muster under the harsh light of what we so fondly refer to in our thoughts as our contemporary nationalistic standards. But it goes without saying, this notwithstanding, that you cannot judge yesterday's failure by today's success. To postulate the direct negation of this would be to go too far and to currently commit a travesty against the race of mankind and, of course, speech itself. Yet speak one must, and this quite obviously means me. My statement is this—more

125

latitude would be more than welcome. At that time, and since, even I, at my utmost, was not privy to enough information. Therefore, I can, as is understood, speak only without the benefit of diametric contradiction, unless more is expected of me, in which event I would not be adverse to holding myself, and the other panelists in my party, in substantial abeyance, both now and otherwise. Little, or even less, will it profit us, I think, nor the generation to come after us and to cross-index us, to offer each other various personal and sundry opinions disproportionately or needlessly. Trust, we can agree, is paramount, now as never before. It is on this account, and only on this account, that knowledge of the facilities must be tolerated if not lauded. Persons to have come before my ken, which, admittedly, is and was the limited ken of the patient, deserved every consideration as one professional to another. Nevertheless, although I was not sick, nor even under suspicion by those responsible for oversight, I was cared for. My debt is great. I would mention the name, but there are legal reasons. Suffice it to say, due reference has been made in the writings of others as well as can be expected by us and by our detractors, both preponderantly and effectively. The answer is inescapable, not only for the time being, but also for the good of the community. May God protect us. We can do no more nor do no less. Meekly, mildly, and with consciousness aforethought, neither I nor my family bears them any ill will in the slightest. Speaking in summation, then, as one who has spoken the truth as God has given him the light to do it, let me correct your faulty impression

and hasten to beg that reciprocity be your watchword, too.
Or also.

Now, if I might turn my attention to Nurse Jones.

Now, if we were to turn our attention to Nurse Jones.

Now, if you will turn your attention to Nurse Jones.

(A cognomen surely.)

WHAT MY MOTHER'S FATHER WAS REALLY THE FATHER OF

1

These are the things she said to me.

2

My mother said her father was as big as a battleship, as big as a building—a horse, she said that her father was as big as a horse, and also as strong as one, too.

3

My mother said that her father was a giant of a man, that he was a regular six-footer, that people were always shouting up at him to try to get him to look down at them and maybe be their friend. She said that people were always shouting, "Hey, Mister Six-Footer, tell us what the weather is like up there? Is it already snowing?"

4

My mother said total strangers couldn't get over it, the tallness and the strongness of her father. She said complete strangers were always passing comment on it. She said, "Not like with some people I could name." She said, "With some people I could name, they go into a room, no one gives them the first courtesy of even taking any notice. You would not, with some people, even know that they are there at all."

5

My mother said, "Stand up. Look like you are somebody. Try to look like you are trying to amount to something. Show them who you are. Make believe you are who you say you are. Are you putting your best foot forward? Put your best foot forward. Show them that you intend to be a member in good standing. My father was a member in good standing."

6

She said that anyone could look and see that her father was a person of unquestionable refinement. She said, "You don't have to take my word for it." She said, "Ask anyone." She said, "Why should I all by myself have to be the whole judge and jury?" She said, "Why stand on ceremony? You can go ahead and satisfy your curiosity any time you want." She said, "I can wait. I've got the patience. I've got more than enough patience for the both of us." She said, "Believe me, I've got enough patience for the whole country of China and also for his brother Siam."

7

She said, "You name the language, he could talk it." She said, "Where was the man's nose?" She said, "The answer is it was forever in a book." She said, "There was no telling what the man might have made of himself if God had only given him a decent interval to do it in, if God had only let my father live like anybody else."

8

My mother said that her father was the Father of the Steam Engine and of the Refrigerator and of certain other creations, but that the stinking Gentiles came in and took advantage of the man's good nature and stole all of the blueprints from him, so that now you wouldn't find the proof of it not anywhere in the world, nowhere on earth was there a way to get the proof of all of the things that my mother's father was really the father of.

9

You know what she said? She said that with just his little finger he could have broken every bone in all of their whole stinking rotten Gentile bodies, but that the man was too refined of a person to lower himself down to their filthy dirty stinking rotten level and let anybody catch him stooping to do it.

10

She said it broke her father's heart, the way they all stole from him, the Gentiles and the Irish and the landlords. She said, "But you know what? The man would not retaliate. The man would not do it, not for one filthy dirty stinking rotten instant."

11

My mother said, "Listen to me, I am here to tell you, the man was a saint, and that is what killed him."

12

She said, "Take one guess who you remind me of." She said, "Because *that* is who you remind me of."

13

She said, "You know what you are?" She said, "You are too decent, you are too sweet-natured."

14

She said, "I am going to tell you the truth—you are too good for your own good."

15

My mother said, "A creature like you, how could it expect to fend for itself?" She said, "A person has to be a bully, a roughneck, a criminal, a hoodlum."

16

She said, "I know you, I'm no fool—wild horses could not make you get down with them on their filthy dirty stinking rotten lousy level."

17

She said, "Throwbacks, that's what I call them. I call them throwbacks—and you know what else? I am not ashamed to say so to their face."

18

She said, "Don't think I don't know." She said, "I promise you, I could give the whole gang of them lessons."

19

She said, "You want to hear something?" She said, "Sit yourself down for two seconds and I will tell you something." She said, "I had to be made of iron."

20

When my mother got old and sick, she said that when she was a little girl in an orphanage, that they gave out bread and jam in the orphanage, that they gave it out every day at three o'clock, and that she always ate hers the instant they gave it out, but that her big sister Helen didn't, that her big sister Helen saved the bread and jam that they had given out, and that her big sister Helen always put hers away somewhere for later, but that later, when my mother got too hungry to wait for supper anymore, that her big sister Helen would go get the bread and jam that she had been saving and that every day she did this, that every day my mother's big sister Helen would save her bread and jam and then come running with it to give it to my mother when my mother was hungry and had eaten up hers.

21

When my mother got older and sicker, she said that sometimes the streetcar would come banging up the hill at the same time the clock was banging three o'clock in the orphanage, and that she thought that if you could hear both of them going outside and inside at once, that then it was a secret sign which said that you were going to get a visit, that getting off of the streetcar here comes one or the other of them, your mother or your father, but that there never, not once, was either one of them for her, not either her mother or her father. And that then when it wasn't, that she remembered he was dead.

22

My mother said, "That's why I had to have my big sister's bread and jam."

23

She said, "Mine wasn't ever any good anymore because of being cried on it."

24

Listen to me—you know what my mother told me once when she thought she was going to pass away?

25

My mother said that her big sister Helen wasn't really the one who was the older one and that their father just went away.

26

So much for his brother Siam.

THE DOG

I was never in a place like that. I was an American boy
when they had places like that. So everything I say is just
me imagining things. Except for the names, of course. I
know the names. I have a list. I have been making a list.
You couldn't guess the names I already have on it. But I
have not even scratched the surface yet. There is just no
telling what it is going to take for me to get the list completed.
Because the point of this is that they only want you to hear
about a handful. They only want you to hear about the
same ones which they want you to hear about, which are
the same ones everybody all over the world has already
heard about. Whereas there were secret ones. There were
hundreds of them. Even hundreds is a big understatement.
They had them everywhere. You couldn't guess where they
had secret ones. You would faint dead-away if I told you
where they had some of them. You would think what a liar
I was if I told you, or was crazy or was worse.

Here is one of the famous ones that is known to absolutely everybody.

Ravensbrück.

You probably heard of that one.

I think it sounds like a name.

Not like Oswiecim.

Imagine having to say Oswiecim morning, noon, and night. That is probably why they called it Auschwitz, even though Auschwitz wasn't its real name.

But take my real name.

I should put my name on my list.

What if they had a barber at Treblinka, at Buchenwald, at Dachau? I have been thinking about this. What if they had to have a barber to get all of the hair off of them for when the women came and the girls came—get off all of their hair everywhere—didn't they do that, take off their hair for something, didn't they take it all off of the girls and off of the women for some terrible purpose?

So they must have had a person who did it. They must have had a person who cut the hair off. It must have been a person who would be good at it, and who would not get tired from doing it and who would know how to keep doing it, just cutting and cutting and not giving the wrong answers. Because look at how hard it would be just to keep doing it, you would have to be a one-hundred-percent professional— all of those girls coming in at you and taking their clothes off and all of those women coming in at you and taking their clothes off, and your job is to keep on cutting their

138

hair off without letting them think that you are doing it for any other reason other than the one that it is all for their own good—to help them keep clean, to help them keep their health up, to save them all of the bother of washing it and of combing.

So what do you think about the question of who did it?

You think they would give the job to what kind of a person?

Tell me which gender, at least, and how old in years you would want this person to be.

Between 1938 and 1944, I made regular visits in from Long Island to my father's place of business. It wasn't just my father's business. It was his business in business with his brothers. It was the business of making hats for women and then of getting Macy's and Gimbel's to buy them in big quantities just to begin with. My father would show me around to all of his workers and then call up for his barber to come up to give me a haircut, and a man came up and did it.

Then this is what my father would say.

"Now that you've been cleaned up, let's go out and put on the dog."

Then my father would give the man the money and take me out to a Longchamps for lunch and then, later on, to DePinna's for something new, like new leggings.

The money my father gave the barber, here is how he did it.

He slipped it to him.
You know, slipped it—a way you work the hand.

Birkenau.
Carthage.
Oz.
New York.

KNOWLEDGE

She said, You want me to kiss it and make it well? Come
sit and I will kiss it and make it well. Come let me see it
and I will kiss it and make it well. Just take your hand
away from it and let me just look. I promise you, I am just
going to look. Oh, grow up, could looking make it worse?
Do us both a favor and let me look. I swear, all I am going
to do is to look. So is that it? Are you telling me that's it?
That can't be it. Are you sure that's it? You're not really
telling me that that is what all of this fuss is about. Is that
what all of this fuss is about? I cannot believe that that is
what all of this fuss is about. Is that what you have been
making such a fuss about? Don't tell me that that is what
you have been making all of this fuss about. You call that
something? That's not something. That's nothing. You know
what that is? I want to tell you what that is. That is nothing.
Does it hurt? It doesn't hurt. It couldn't hurt. Why do you
say it hurts? How could you say it hurts? You really want

141

me to believe it hurts? Is that what you are telling me, you are telling me that it hurts? Because I cannot believe that that is what you are really telling me, that you are really telling me that a thing like that could hurt. A little thing like that could not conceivably hurt. Do us both a favor and don't tell me it hurts. So when I do this, does it hurt? What makes you say it hurts? Are you sure it hurts? How could it hurt? Give me one good reason why it should hurt. I should show you something that really hurts. I am going to give you some advice. You want some advice? Count your lucky stars you don't have something that really hurts. You know what you are doing? Let me tell you what you are doing. I want you to sit here and hear me tell you exactly what you are doing. Because guess what. You are making something out of nothing. You want me to tell you what you are doing? Because that is what you are doing, you are making something out of nothing. So don't act like you didn't know. You know what? You're not doing yourself any good when you put on such an act. I am amazed at you, putting on such an act. So how come you never figured this out for yourself? You should have figured this out for yourself. Why should you, of all persons, not be the one to figure this out for yourself? I want you to promise me something—next time try to figure things out for yourself.

Forget it.

I do not need anybody to promise me anything.

Let me ask you something.

No, definitely again you better skip it.

The answer would make me sick.

Listen, you know what is wrong with you? Because there is something very, very, very wrong with you. I guarantee you, I promise you, a person's mother knows.

BEHOLD THE
INCREDIBLE REVENGE
OF THE SHIFTED P. O. V.

How shall we say the clock was bought and paid for? For surely the seller's sticker on the thing declared a figure remarkably bolder than these youngsters could decently manage. But they were so keen, the two of them, and so ungovernable in their zeal. Of what earthly pertinence was it that their purse could scarce stand up to the mild demands of the humblest item in this shop? And the clock, oh my, as to its forbidding tariff, great heavens, this, please be clear, was certain to be seen by most shoppers as another, and much harsher, matter entirely. But what, pray tell, did other matters, certain or otherwise, have to do with anything when it was naught but the pressure of necessity itself that rested its infinite weight on the stunned hearts of these young people? For there the clock stood in its stony oaken case, all solemnity in its ancient bearing (after all, the sticker stated "Early Nineteenth Century" no less forthrightly than it stated price) as it spoke its artful speech of sturdiness, of continuity, of permanence, promising to deliver these affiliations first and therefore, when the time was right, everything else.

It said it could confer as much.

Or so we heard it pledge its word to the new homemakers.

"Wow, that's no joke!" the boy announced with some excessive gusto, meaning to exaggerate his amazement not just for the good fun of making fun of himself but also to suggest to the shop's proprietor—who had hovered into position—that, in fact, for these two customers, the amount would be no large sum at all.

"But only think of it!" the girl exclaimed. "I mean, wouldn't it be like an heirloom really? I mean, when we have a family, couldn't we just sort of pass it on to them the way real people do, sort of like generations upon generations forever?"

The boy colored at his spouse's high sentence, wanting to hasten to correct her where it had struck his ear that the girl had gone with it, great Christ, a measure or two too far. But the boy knew the damage had been done, that it was always already centuries too late ever to withdraw the smallest wrongness, that the proprietor—the man hovering ever more tellingly into position—a lofty enough presence to hover, actually—had heard all, judged all— "generations upon generations forever" indeed!—doubtlessly savoring the evidence on a tongue that would publish conclusions elsewhere.

Ah, God, the boy could hear the verdict carrying down the ages after him: "Innocent young dear has gone and got itself a goodish burden, now hasn't it? Dreadful silly sap."

That did it, or so it seems not unsafe for us to suppose.

At any rate, grinning horribly, the boy motioned for the girl to fetch the "family" checkbook from her handbag— so that, by whatever means fiscal, the clock was got—and a note was accordingly made and thereafter wired to the fancy key that poked from the fancy keyhole whose lock could let you get at the lordly pendulum either for the business of starting it up or, if ever required, shutting it down.

SOLD.

And so forth and so on.

We are reporting the clock was theirs.

A "grandmother clock" was what status the clock was rendered by the reference books in which its kind was pictured, this, it is not unlikely, in pursuit of a program to restrain the thing to a rank not so grand at all—and though the provenance of the clock was very probably more local than not, still (the seller had seemed so tall, so hovering, so . . . *otherly*), once the clock had taken up its post against their bedroom wall (there was really nowhere else for them to fit the clock, what with the premises being—the marriage was hardly yet out of its cradle—so cruelly unbaronial), the owners succumbed to the practice of engaging the phrase "our imported piece" whenever inquiries were made by one or another young couple who, after very persuasive fare indeed, at the card table set up for the purpose in the kitchen, were escorted back into the bedroom for a bit of TV with their coffee and their dessert and their cordials.

"Oh, but it's so unutterably special," the other wife would say. "No wonder you want it back here where you sleep, where a chic antique of its type can really be better appreciated on a much more frequent basis."

"Yeah, nice," the other husband would say. "So you guys inherit it from your families or something?"

But whatever enthusiasms the other young couple would offer to the ethers as they bit into cake and drank from goblets and sipped from cups no bigger than big thimbles, sooner or later someone would be bound to observe—generally when the clock's imperturbable chimes were finally being heard from—that the time was the better part of an hour fast.

Or slow.

But wrong.

Fast or slow but wrong.

Always wrong.

Never not anything but chaotically wrong.

Off.

Way off.

Not right.

Not once.

Not anywhere even close.

There was no remedy for it.

Years into the marriage, the thing still tolled the hour nowhere near the hour—and when one went to the living room (oh, as they will to all couples who accomplish the early stewardship of a magisterial object, other important objects had issued to our couple, even a commodious enough living room had) to see what time it was, one had to smack one's head and reinstruct oneself that for such a use, for telling the time, the clock was no good at all. Whereupon, whichever of them it was, that party would then get himself prayerfully down onto his knees, would work the fancy key, would draw open the panel whose business it was to keep from view the relentless commerce of the pendulum, would put a finger out to stop it, would then reset the whole affair, hideously mindful all the while that whatever adjustment was being made will have long since, hours hence, begun to yield to the mischief transferring exacting correction into more and more violent error.

The bother was pointless.

Clock people were summoned from other counties, from distant precincts, from bizarre neighborhoods, wild sullen grisly creatures, who, lavishly bearded and extravagantly undeterred, brought with them impossibly exotic instruments and, sometimes, wordless ghostly staring children, their fathers keeping to their dismal labors for days without sleep, taking no recesses for food even—greasy oblongs of oil-dark canvas spread out all around as the place more and more accumulated the parts of . . . *our imported piece!*— the thing nauseatingly sundered, undone, suddenly truly charmlessly alien, whatever the truth of its origin.

No help.

Nothing worked.

The clock kept keeping the wrong time.

But no one is saying that it was ever a stroke less reassuring to look upon.

He who looked upon the clock was reassured.

She, too.

Made present to the sacrament of things going on, of no change.

It was okay.

The children had come and gone.

To be sure, the notion of the generations was just beginning to exert itself good and proper the year the couple packed up and gave up the place where the marriage had conducted its offspring into the habits that had been proclaimed for it. So here was the time for something smaller and more manageable, for a dwelling better fitted to the compressions of middle age—and the clock went to that dwelling with them, of course—all the time in the world for passing the clock along to the first one to wed—no, to the first one to honor the ceremonies of homemaking—no yet again, to the first one to express the resolution to prostrate himself and spouse before a token of the household, consenting to welcome the instruction the clock would give.

But, look, see how we, the tellers of what is told, are not exempt from what is said.

Behold, must not the clock keep perfect time before the story can be a story?

And so it does!

All day.

And all the next ones, too.

Magic.

How else to explain?

The spontaneous institution of what was helplessly wanted—everything in impeccable working order—nothing even a tick's hair off.

Go ahead, call the time-keepers, get in touch with the official custodians, telephone from right in there—I mean, from right in there in the little sleeping room the widow and I have now taken to storing the clock in and to keeping tidied and readied for the visits of our children's children's children.

You'll see.

Say, "Could you please tell me what time it is, please?"

Now watch the clock.

Right on the money, yes?

But here is the thing.

Every time the old woman and I hear it chiming the time it really is, a ridiculous condition of terror takes up our minds in its hands and twists. I mean, the clock, the good old clock—our very index of the durable order of things— has got us scared stiff.

151

ON THE BUSINESS OF
GENERATING TRANSFORMS

I have, for example, heard such sentences as "They didn't know what each other should do" . . .

NOAM CHOMSKY

He did not mean in Ahnenerbe, in Ahmecetka, in Ananiev, in Apion, Arad, Armyansk, Artemovsk, Aumeier, Auschwitz, Baden, Bad Tölz, Baetz, Ballensiefen, Balti, Belzec, Beresovka, Bergen-Belsen, Bessarabia, Birkenau, Blizyn, Bobruisk, Bolzano, Borisov, Borispol, Brabag, Bratislava, Breendonck, Breslau, Brest Litovsk, Buchenwald, Budzyn, Bukovina, Chelmno, Chisinau, Chmiolnik, Chortkov, Cservenka, Czestochowa, Dachau, Dorohoi, Dorohucza, Dubno, Flir, Florstedt, Flossenbürg, Gomel, Gorlitz, Grodno, Hilversum, Kamenka, Karlovac, Karsava, Kaunas, Kharkov, Kirovograd, Kislovodsk, Kistarcsa, Klimovichni, Koblenz, Kobryn, Kodyma, Kopkow, Kowel, Krakow-Placzow,

Krzemienec, Kulmhof, Kummer, Kurhessen, Kursk, Kysak, Kyustendil, Langleist, Larissa, Lida, Liscka, Litzenberg, Ljubljana, Lodz, Lom, Lublin, Lvov, Majdanek, Malkinia, Mariupol, Mielec, Mitrovica, Mogilev, Moldavia, Monowitz, Nasielek, Neu-Sandez, Nevel, Novo Moskovsk, Novo Ukrainka, Olshanka, Opitz, Oppeln, Oswiecim, Pionki, Plovdiv, Poltava, Poniatowa, Poznan, Pristina, Pskov, Raschwitz, Ravensbrück, Rawa-Ruska, Regensburg, Rovno, Saarbrücken, Saarpflaz, Salonika, Sambor, Sdolbunov, Silesia, Simferopol, Skopje, Slavyansk, Slivina, Slovakia, Slovenia, Slutsk, Sluzk, Smolensk, Snigerevka, Snovsk, Sobibor, Sonsken, Struma, Staden, Stammlager, Stettin, Szarva, Szeged, Szolnok-Doboka, Taganrog, Tallin, Târgu-Mures, Tarnopol, Tartu, Theresienstadt, Tighina, Timisoara, Tiraspol, Tizabogdany, Tomaschow, Transnistria, Trawniki, Treblinka, Trikkala, Trzynietz, Turck, Turda, Uzhorod, Vapniarka, Varna, Vijnita, Vilna, Vinnitsa, Vitebsk, Vitezka, Volhynia-Podolia, or in Vyazma, or in Zakopane, or in Zangen, or in Zupp.

But, yes, certainly it is probably true that they did not know what each other should do. They probably did not even know what they themselves should.

FISH STORY

As far as I was always concerned, the outdoors was where
you maybe went when it wasn't raining and only when you
had to. I wasn't the only indoorsy type in my parish to
cherish this unhealthy opinion. One thing was, you couldn't
hear *Jack Armstrong* under some spreading chestnut tree—
because Jewish boys did not have spreading chestnut trees
and, anyway, back in those burnished days, portable radios
went about three pounds shy of the total tonnage of the
Normandie, crew and cargo loaded. Or maybe they hadn't
even invented them yet—portable radios, I mean, not Jewish boys. But the days were indeed burnished, all right,
aglow with the feeble light those darling flame-shaped amber
bulbs struggled to give off. Everybody's mother thought
they were the cat's pajamas, those cunning bulbs, just the
thing for the fake-Tudor houses everybody lived in. Oh, we
were all as happy as clams in those glowy places the mothers
tried to pry us from into the bright outdoorsy day calling
all unwholesome boys. All you wanted weekdays was a box

of Uneeda Biscuits or a row of Walnettos, to sustain you from *Jack Armstrong* through *Lorenzo Jones.* Saturdays, *Let's Pretend* and *Grand Central Station* so filled the inner kid and stilled the organs of ingestion, you went serenely, the whole day, without. Sundays we won't even talk about, so that you will not have to hear what it sounds like when a grown man sobs. Oh, I suppose I can risk a little bit, mention just *The Adventures of Nick Carter, Master Detective,* and *Quick as a Flash,* and leave it, I think, impressively at that.

Are you kidding me—the outdoors? The outdoors was for droolers and for nose-pickers, for kids called Buster and Butch and the one, I swear, called Bix. Outdoors was for the kid we called "Wedge" because someone told us the wedge was your simplest tool.

But sometimes God was merciless and it did not rain.

It was then that the mothers came armed with reminders of Green Harvey, to storm the trenches of Bad Hygiene.

But first they'd move into action with rickets.

You'll get rickets!

(Aw, Ma, what's rickets?)

Rickets is from not playing outdoors and from eating meat from a can! Do I ever give you meat from a can?

(Aw, Ma, I've got to stay tuned for a coded message.)

Tell me something, Mr. Young-Man-Who-Is-Willing-To-Break-A-Mother's-Blood-Vessel, have you lately taken a good look at Harvey Joel Rosensweig?

Visions of Green Harvey four houses down always did the ruthless trick. Because you did not want to look like

156

Harvey Joel Rosensweig anymore than Harvey Joel Rosensweig did. And if you were the sort of chicken-hearted
impressionable that I was, the mother in question did not
have to break a blood vessel. You want to prise a believer
away from the family Emerson, you will never get a better
crowbar than Visions of Green Harvey. But this, of course,
was back when liddlies were just little.

And that was another thing they hadn't invented yet—
smart kids. Not only that, but they also hadn't *un*invented
parents who never heard of traumatizing the crap out of a
ten-year-old global idiot.

Green Harvey!

You never saw a kid quicker when it came to buckling
on his swashes.

So there you were, on the lawn, just crazy to participate
in the American Way of Life. You had the Wheaties box to
guide you in the modalities of how your American boy is
supposed to play, but what you didn't have was anybody
to do it with—because that was the day it was your mother
who was the only mother home to hound her issue into the
streets, all of the other mothers being at the neighborhood
rummy game, where it is that the mothers in a perfect world
were always meant to be.

I'd sit on the curb for a time and stare at some glinty
thing in the gutter. I don't know what it was with me, but
in those burnished days, whenever I sat on a curb, that is
what I would do, cut my eyes sideways from side to side
until I had spotted some shining thing, a bonanza in the

gutter. Then I'd sit there, at whatever distance, trying to guess what it was. Not *guess*, really, but just declare aloud with mad conviction—because the point was that you were always something magical, Renfrew of the Royal Mounties or Sergeant Preston of the Yukon, alone like this, the star-tling powers in you something scary in your solitude, and you of course would just simply *know* whatever it was, off there in the gutter—not even needing a second glint.

Gum wrapper!

And then I'd get up and go look.

The time's too burnished for me to remember if I ever guessed right. But I remember one day what it was when I'd guessed wrong, and it is this which accounts for my getting into this whole outdoorsy business with you in the first place.

Because one day it was a fishhook.

Now a fishhook in the gutter was not a discovery you routinely made in the gutters of the streets where I come from. I'm talking about a place called the Five Towns, a sort of way-station along the ongoing Diaspora about twenty miles out on Long Island, counting from the center of familial concern—which was the New York City where all of the fathers bravely went each day with their brown suits and their gray hats.

I wasn't all that dumb about fishing, mind you. Not only did I know it was a thing the Wheaties box okayed, but I knew that almost all the grammar-school readers had Skippy always doing it with his dad, or Bucky always wanting to do it with his pa, or Franklin Delano Roosevelt always doing it with his dog.

I knew they all did it with an animal they called a worm and with a stick they called a pole.

I knew they got *worm* and *line* and *pole*, and then where they went with them was to a *crick*.

I wasn't too sure we had anything around there where we lived that would qualify as a crick, but the first three items I figured for a cinch. Hook in hand—you know, *holding* it—my mother's shrieked philosophy conjuring the shout of calamity in my ear (*You will put an eye out with that thing!*), I headed for the garage, happy to be in darkness for the time it took to get the pole (a piece of picket fence, an upright left over because the lawn we had did not go that far) and the line (a bunch of Venetian-blind cord the vermin had set up for themselves as a haven in a heartless world).

Worm.

Worm?

I'd seen a few in my time. But not really where they had come from. I mean, a worm was something Green Harvey would come running at you with—until you had seen him coming and took off a safe distance the other way, far enough for his fat to make him quit coming and eat it—the worm. But it never crossed my mind to wonder where Harvey Joel Rosensweig got his worm from. I suppose I just leaped to the conclusion you had to be a Green Harvey to get one.

Worm! Worm! Worm!

I think I remember scuffing up the pebbles in our drive-

way for a trice or two, giving many maddening seconds to
my idea of how a real American boy breasts all hardship
to quest the great quest. What I mean is that I was by this
time back in those burnished days pretty damn wised-up
as to a pessimist's construction of everything—meaning: if
I did not catch a fish, I would be the last one to be surprised
I didn't. It was a boyhood perpendicular to the kind you
read about in the readers in school. It was a boyhood where
the community prepared for disaster and was amazed when
it did not strike. It was a boyhood where standards were
sky-high but where expectation had been leached out of
them to make a safely null class. Hey, I'm not whining—I
am just giving you the whole heart-rending picture.

So here we are, nostalgia fans, back behind the family
garage, with a piece of picket fence, about nine feet of
chewed-up Venetian-blind cord, and a hook Satan had set
out to do temptation's work there in a gutter-looker's gutter.

It took about a half hour to walk it to the crick, an inlet
(let out by the Atlantic Ocean) spanned by a little bridge
you crossed to get to the beach clubs. We called that inlet
The Inlet, and we called the bridge The Bridge—not un-
mindful of how Skippy and Bucky were always coming up
with these really great names for things—it dawning on me
that if you got yourself out there on a little poke of dock
up on out there on the landward side (hello, Skippy! hello,
Bucky!), you could drop a line down into water deep enough.

Listen, I can appreciate how knot-tying is probably a
pretty big deal to most people, but for me there's never

been much in it after the shoelace stage. So if you are
wondering how I got that Venetian-blind cord stuck onto
that piece of picket fence, save your worry for the hook.
Because the hook, jeez, it truly was a bitch. I mean, I tried
a lot of very fancy thinking, but my brain could only handle
the thinking that it definitely could not be done unless you
had a derrick. So I just dropped my line in, tossed my
Venetian-blind cord in, hookless but serious-looking if you
went by the principle of its having lifted up and lowered
back down again lots of busy slats.

So how else could this all come out but as a good and
countervailing lesson for a boy who always waited for the
worst?

I am not saying that what happened converted an indoors
type to an outdoors one. I still get closest to God somewhere
where you can control the light. But I will just say that I
went ahead and I pulled up no fewer than a dozen lunatic
fish with that stick of picket fence—fish that just bit anywhere *all at once* on that Venetian-blind cord and would
not let go of wherever they'd bit on a bet.

I did not take even one of them home to prove it, though.
As a matter of fact, I did not even take one of them off the
line. I just dropped that stick of fence and ran like hell,
all twelve or so of those infectious things still on there fas-
tened to it, their killer jaws clamped there in a kid-killing
grin.

Oh, I can see how it is probably true that Green Harvey might have stuck around—the loon might even have

harvested those evil-hearted monstrosities, to pitch one through the window of every mother's son who had ever believed himself to be far enough away from harm indoors. But I had had my fair squint at what is sometimes under outdoor things, and I knew that I did not want to really know what was.

It was better than thirty years later, when I was turning the pages of a Ladybird Book for an indoors type of my own (a kid whose peaceable opinion of nature continues to treacherously thrive on an abundance of urban ignorance), that I found out what it was that the Wheaties box had got me into back when my heart was still brave and true— namely, the worst scare ever to chase me through all of the burnish of my youth.

It was just a blowfish.

They were just blowfish—every last one of them all blown up.

He'll bite on any fool thing, your silly blowfish will. But so, for that matter, will your friendly reader—hook, line, and sinker. I mean, since it is all the same in the end, and if it is all the same to you, give me human nature every time—and the equally hideous fishing of men.